LOWER HEAVEN

Episode One:
I, of the Storm

By Benjamin Loomis
Published and Distributed by Free Radical Books

Viva la!
Lets git it.

I

Behold Felix, fumbling to roll his dawn cigarette. His rat's nest head looks ready to roll off his shoulders, bones barely keeping him upright in the bus seat, the complexion of a man twice his age. He is hung over, and every bash of the brakes sends a spray of ribboned tobacco catapulting onto his lap. He tries for a minute more, rips his paper, gives up.

"Man, I swear these buses get shakier every month." he says, mouth dusty.

His friend Vic, one bus seat over, thrust a cock-eyed look at him, the only kind he had. A childhood veteran of the turf wars that raged through the Causeway housing projects and mangier bits of the island-city, the face of Felix's friend was hatched with scars across his forehead and oft-busted nose. Untreated snakepox as a kid gave his cheeks and scruff chin a nibbled look.

When shirtless, his wiry torso was a scatterplot of daggerholes from his gutter upbringing. In one fateful alley scuffle long ago, Vic had caught a brick-sock upside the head that cracked his left orbital, the eye had never set right again. He could still see from it, but it dawdled and wandered, leaving the other side of his face rigid with overcorrected muscle. The same, golden hit had snapped off one of his front teeth, giving him a hole to spit through and make disapproving sounds with.

"Its ye hands bruv, dis bus ting ent moved inna minute."

2

"Ah."

"Cummon, were wastin daylite. Lets git it." he said, scowling out the bus window.

Vic grabbed his parachute sack and piled out of the packed vehicle, knowing Felix would follow after groaning. They picked through the traffic to the sidewalk and began forcing through the pedestrians, inward to the city. The bus had at least gotten them off the stone bridge of Merit Causeway where they lived, and onto the island proper.

"Dis *foookin* festival traffick bruv!" Vic said, turning back briefly as he cricked his neck and hoisted his hood against the rainy season drizzle. They picked around the blocked intersection, feeling miniscule. The highrises rose on all sides, matching every person with a ton of cement. Temporary fences and warning flags diverted the normal flow of the street, turning the thoroughfare into a worksite. Inside, between the slow flowing puddles accumulating in the cobbles, Civic Workers young and old were hard at work with festival preparations. Functionary Square was always a site on the parade route, which meant it was a mess of tarpaulin-covered effigies and half-built bleachers for weeks before, making transit from the Causeway neighborhoods into lower Heaven more abominable than usual.

Every year the Festival grew louder and grander, more bombastic in its patriotism. It needed to. There were two centuries of festivals before this one to top. The upcoming Festival of the Free, commemorating the 244th birthday of the City, was primed to be the biggest, free-est celebration ever.

For three whole days at the end of the wet season, the whole city went on unpaid holiday to remember the day the City's Founders, against universal odds, survived the journey over the Poison Sea and crash-landed on the lake-island they now called home. This disparate pack of refugees spread their gaze on the barren rock they had found, and named it Heaven. Over the next two centuries they had become its pantheon, their faces, words, and ideas of government elevated to a near sacred level.

The Founders had fled the Old Continent— a horrid place, the History Book said. Life there was tyranny and oppression, ill-blooded dynasties and unending, machine warfare that molested the fallow earth until it could feed nothing. Those times were unspeakably dark. Apparently. No others had ever come across the Sea after them.

Probably because the journey had been suicidal. No one knew at the time what lay behind the vast dark ocean. They sailed out on seven massive flying ships, the Arks, propelled by a mythical liquid fuel that the Old Continent had used to build its cities and then grind them to dust with war.

They expected nothing, as the story went, but feared more than death to remain. By the skin of sublime improbability, and rather surprising to the starving refugees, three of the Arks found something. After watching their sisters dip down into the steaming waters, the last of the old fuel dwindling, the Arks were delivered by miracle into the unknown, a whole new continent, unspoiled, bountiful, green. And on it, they endeavored with their lives to make a place for themselves that rejected everything about their homeland, rebuilding their society from scratch, with the principles and systems they and other seekers had only been able to whisper about in clandestine meetings from whence they came.

They crystallized on three ideas, to create a civilization that honored each person. Those notions became Heaven's

Tripartite Ideals: Merit, Logic, and Freedom for all. These Ideals emitted a noble miasma which every one of the City's governing structures was built on, or at least justified by.

So the Festival of the Free was a little silly, because after two centuries those three words were scant more than the boilerplate on coins and government archways. Even the highest echelons of the Wizard Community acknowledged this emptiness in private, Felix knew. Only simps saw the event as anything but a street-clogging, self-congratulatory show of civic pageantry, designed to repeat the Dream of Heaven to the next generation until they could repeat it to themselves. But after 244 years, Felix reasoned, the Wizards were obligated to make the Festival a little larger every year. What would it say if they didn't?

There were yells as they squeezed between the barricades and temporary worklamps pinching the traffic. Felix glimpsed the hold up. A flatbed autotram loaded with lumber had whinnied over. A soggy brigade of workers in orange coveralls were pulling the beams out of the road. He watched a team of drenched old men, legs ready to buckle, scraping a block off the cobbles that took six to carry. Mixed into the work crew were women and children as well, doing their best. Felix knew that by looking close you could read the numbers tattooed on their necks, so he didn't.

Overseeing the Civic Workers was a contingent of City Corps Rangers in their slick black overcoats, tripartite arm bands, strapshots on wrists, there if the law needed to be kept. Half were commanding the batches of CWs, and the rest fended off the honking, hapless traffic. A Wizard monitor hovered above the scene. He stood in a levitating cloche— a metal-and-glass chamber, domed at the top and flat bottomed like a bell. The transparent bubble sloped the rain off the Wizard, who was supposed to be watching the armed Rangers, but Felix was pretty sure he was reading a paperback instead.

Red mixed into the mud puddles the CWs splashed through, seeping out from the overturned tram. Everyone proceeded at pace, no medicvans were coming. Whoever was underneath that had accepted this as a risk. All of the orange-clad CWs had made the same deal. The Civic Works Program was a social initiative introduced by Wizard visionaries generations ago, to combat the City's then-still-early unemployment problem. It provided anyone who fell to homelessness with a job, a bed, and three square meals a day. In return, you did the work the City assigned you.

The deal had been better before they moved the free housing out to the barges on the lake's edge, back when the worker's planted trees and picked up trash for their service — but overall it was still better than dying of exposure or getting your brainstem reformatted by the next Storm that passed over. Everyone was eligible for the CWP— hence the mixed ages of the work crew. Setting up the Festival was light-work. Anyone more able-bodied was out on the floating farms, or building new Opportunity Housing, or had been assigned other helpful tasks. By volunteering yourself to the CWP (or by being prescribed duty for a crime) you converted yourself to an overhead cost on the municipal ledger for as long as your contract ran, or was renewed. A lot of people ended up turning to the CWP in times of need, and the program had been scaled up recently.The Wizards even threw in a nifty orange jumpsuit and a free bit of body art. Everyone in Heaven was born with a Social Identification Number, but only Civic Workers got to have their SIN tattooed into their neck for free.

Felix sleepily soaked up the scene, gently knowing that CWP work was his destiny in a couple of years if he didn't die some quicker death first. He smiled at it, trying to enjoy his downward spiral for what it was, while it lasted. The bannered words above the workers' heads encouraged all to embrace their roles as defenders of Heaven's virtues. Felix didn't think he'd even defend himself at this point, for what it was he was worth.

"Bruv, wotchutink dem Founders haffa say bout dis? Fookin mess erry year, innit?!" Vic said, brow creased as they pushed through the stymied crowd.

"They'd probably be looking for the nearest Ark and the next continent."

"Tru, prolly."

The two made it through the densest point of the bottleneck and had two meters to themselves.

"Right den—gotta nudda question. Lizzen. Izzit betta bein a slut, or a slave out here den?"

"Are those my only two choices?"

"Basically bruv, yeh."

The two of them passed streetlamp after streetlamp, brightening the dawn's early light coming through Zeliman's Pyramid on their left, one of the Heaven's twelve Colleges. Felix couldn't look up at the blue plate-glass ziggurat, all passive solar leans and overhangs. He didn't have faith he was really even awake, looking around, waiting for reality to kick in. He was still running on autopilot, four hours of sleep and whatever last night had left in his bloodstream. Sometimes this early in the morning he swore he was walking through a fantasy world.

Vic, a bit more ready for the day, fleshed out his premise as they hiked along through the drizzle.

"See blud, we all are, slut orra slave, when it all gits down. All mans gotta work, pay rent, yeah? Most mans out here: *slaves*. Mandem wake up, go ta work, do wot boss-man say. Git fired if ya dont. Same ting, erry time. He tell ya work harda. You say yeh yeh, do a lil more, til he leave, but you dont care, you work byda hour ting— clock-ridin, pullin a good steady slave-wage innit? En bossman dont rilly care, long as *his* bossman happy. He gotta lil slave-wage too, more en you, cuz he manages mans."

"Sounds right."

"I bet. Yer job, blud? At the boot store bruv? *Total* slavin. All the goons ye work wiff. Slave ting. Day in. day out. I ent clownin it, I done worse, bare worse. Ye ent seen a fish-house, bruv, truss me."

"But aren't those just normal jobs?"

"Not if ya goes broke workin em bruv! Only makin the dosh dey let ya, annits nevah enuff. Maybe you useda could, one time. Dats why erryone tinks its just *normal*, innit, but no one out here getting ahead. Alla slaves dont realize. Dey ent even *know* bout the Wuss-Wen bruv."

Vic referred here to the **WSWN**—the Way Shit Was Now. The two of them had talked about it so much they made up an acronym one drunken night. The mutual distrust, the hardness on everyone's eyes, waiting for the next disaster, expecting stagnation at best. Not everyone named it but you could tell they felt it, heard them talk about or around it in different ways. You couldn't avoid it, life in lower Heaven was getting bad, and if you asked anyone older than you, it used to be better.

Felix didn't know if that was true, but it definitely seemed busier than when he was young. Nothing ramped down in the city anymore. Even when the traffic turned the roadways to slow paste, for hours every morning and night, hordes rushed about at their business. They were getting caught in the upwell of it now, themselves adding to the morning crowd going out to begin the day. The avenue was already well-peopled, filling with first-shift workers and the local auteurs who sold coffee, umbrellas, corn flautas, tobacco, good luck candles, bug shrouds, chiclesticks, news rags, lottery tickets, and pigmeat-stuffed croissants to them.

Felix fought to keep his drowsing head up, and his heavy pack from stumbling him into a sidewalk *tortilla* press. He held his breath as he swayed past. The smell of hearty food made him sick this early.

"It juss dont work, dem type jobs, it dont, I done em." Vic continued. "You cant expecta make it, only stay still, or fall behind. Im sayin. An dats wot we been doin bruv. We gotta get in a different lane. You know wot dat means."

"... be sluts?"

"Yeh blud. Peak sluts. Like I say, lass night. We ent workin for no wage no more bruv. We gonnaa take dis freeknifin ting serious, start today. We makin moves. We settin our own prices after today. We takin risk, and gettin rewards. *Beeg* ting bruv, truss."

"Uh huh," inserted Felix.

"Yeh—yeh." his friend went on, amping himself up, "In rallity bruv, we been gettin fooked out here, and we ent gittin nuffin for it. Honest, we been playin the game all the wrong ways."

"Uh huh."

"*Uh huh.*" Vic repeated. He stopped and speared Felix with a Look from his good eye, the right one. He sucked the spot where his front teeth weren't.

"Bruv, will you fookin wake up? Act like ya bout ta be somewhere."

"Bleh, sorry." Felix rattled his head for show. "Those sangrias last night really got me."

"Lightweight." said Vic. "Cummon. Keep up." He forced a few steps ahead, then slowed for Felix, sauntering behind.

Felix really hadn't meant to get drunk last night— but a ten hour shift stocking boot boxes all yesterday made it not even a choice, more of an instinct. And it wasn't all his fault. Vic had come out too, and drank almost as much, and didn't stop him. He shouldn't be surprised at least.

Trying to infuse a little pep into his step, clear the liquid cobwebs, Felix bounced to Vic's side.

"Hey! No worries man, I'm feeling good. We're going to kick ass. All good! We'll pull hella slugs. Not like last time."

Vic puffed out air. "We ent goin for slugs dis time. Like I said." he said, eyes mostly forward.

"Oh. Oh right."

They hit Perimeter Blvd. The crowds were already bad. The incoming Causeway flow injected itself into the uncompromising band of traffic running either way on the flat stone road, which encircled the oblong island Heaven occupied. The street's name was a misnomer now, as several blocks of development had been extended out over sections of the lake.

If Felix looked up, straight down the narrow line of Meridian Avenue, he'd see the Edifice, the City's original College and the high seat of the Academocracy, built into the small mountain in the island's middle, its glassy face staring back— so he didn't look. The Wizards who worked and lived there were Heaven's most elite and learned, the best equipped to make decisions and laws for all the people, ascended by their peers to positions of power, as their level of personal excellence dictated.

The Perimeter/Meridian/Merit Causeway interchange

was more fraught with people than ever. The cross streets jumped like a pot at full boil, everyone in a hurry. The roadway was bricked in here too. The ever present cord of the street, the dense, slow-rolling autocarts delivering goods from one part of the city to another, plus the smaller, solar-magic autos and cabbies that filled all of the space the trucks didn't, made the actual roadway untraversable for those keen to keep both feet.

A heavy sample of Heaven's denizens clotted the wide sidewalks. Unassuming, bespectacled professionals swept past hunched clusters of hand-tatted Causeway kids tribed up on the corner. Couriers on all manner of one, two, and three-wheeled vehicles sliced between each. Merit Causeway was adjacent to the South Bank as well, so you got a lot of Zuri— the broad name for the hundreds of native tribes that occupied all of the jungle lands surrounding the lake. Early on, right after the First Settlement, some enterprising Zuri tribesman had encamped on the island's southwest crescent, forming a new colony of their own. This unresolved city planning issue remained so until Heaven's borders grew to encapsulate the South Bank, also known as the Zuri Quarter, and questions arose around how much space the indigenous settlement really needed.

Felix scanned for any big clusters of totem outfits— panther capes, squawkodile masks, phoenix feathers— the ceremonial garms Zuri youth gangs put on prior to committing political actions. He didn't dislike Zuri people, he had nothing against them. But with the WSWN, with all the rage bubbling around the South Bank, you had to stay alert.

They battled left, north, down Perimeter. Above the people and buildings they could see the Aeromobiles, lifting off and touching down from their morning's destination.

Through the churning, Felix had been working on a new problem: he inferred from context that they were doing something different than usual, on this next journey into the jungle. Vic must have told him at some point this week, but the space in his mind where the details should be was an embarrassing opaque fuzz. Not knowing what they were about to parachute out of a flying vehicle to go do was a pinch unnerving as well. He used his lack of info to try and discover two things at once.

"Hey, so... we're not *not* going after slugs this time *because* of last time, are we?"

"Nah."

"Because those cliff ropes can get tangled really easily and take all day to untwist, and I know that now."

"You prolly should know dat bruv, but nah. Not you. Wot I said. Slugs are easy, yeh? Steady buyahs, low sells, any mook can do it. Basic slave work, innit? Dis a new *wavei* for us bruv. Dis new ting gonna nab some real dosh. Stacks bruv, *loots*. Like I said last night."

"Right." Felix said, no closer. Which was actually fine, no matter. Felix was a firm believer that nothing really mattered at all in the world, but this especially. Vic was the licensed Jungle Ranger here. He'd shot Felix's suggestions down a number of times in the previous, which was fair, because Felix knew nothing about hunting that his friend hadn't taught him. So it really didn't matter what they were going after or what he thought of it, and he was perfectly fine with that. The less of his brain he had to use, the better. He was just along for the ride, providing moral support, observational humor and all that.

"Yep. And if all goes well, everyting is just fine, truss me. 'snot you." Vic said, as Felix turned to cross the street.

He hitched his shoulder and kept walking, making a two-note sucking sound with his teeth at Felix, getting him to follow.

"Dis way for a sec mate. Were buyin us a Gooli."

II

The Aero Yard lay behind a high fortressed fence, spiked at intervals with control towers, their roofs a-flip with colored semaphore flags. The hubbub of souls on the block was flattened by the noise of an Aero firing its rotors every minute or so, the silver-hulled bulks jumping the height of four stories with a start, levelling to a bee's hover, before sliding up and forward into the sky as if pulled by a string.

Vic kept walking like he knew where he was going, Felix followed. When they reached the corner of the Yard's palisade fence, they picked their way across the crosswalk and kept straight, so that the slatted barrier was now an arm's length to their left. Across the street from them, the block-and-timber structures that marked Heavenite architecture were spersed with Zilladon hide shelters of warty leather, dye hues making them look like huge sleeping creatures. Some were splayed open, as stores or little cantinas. They strolled on the edge of the Zuri Quarter proper now, a few blocks in and the road system would totally disappear into an uncharted, shuffling sea of tents.

"Mebbe if dey built some real houses, nobody would wanna clear em out." Vic muttered off-hand. It was something he'd said before. Felix just grunted, having no real opinion.

They reached the far corner of the Aero Yard, where it shot off the edge of the island on an artifice of concrete piers. They marched towards an open divot on the opposite corner block, the opening of a large orange tent that formed a courtyard, where Zuri were known to hire themselves out to Rangers and other adventurers outbound on a jungle hunt.

"So, we're bringing someone else?" Felix said as they crossed the street.

"Yeh." Vic said. "S'time."

"Okay, cool. Hey, you want s kebab for breakfast?" Felix said, his stomach starting to yearn.

An immediate, negative, reflexive sound came out of Vic's mouth.

"Ye got dosh for one bruv?" he spat.

"I mean, not til I get paid again," Felix said, backing off.

"Den ye shouda et at home, innit? Pull an apple outta my pack. En dont worry. A *Gooli* guides gonna double, triple up wot we bring home usual."

"Yeah, but what does one of those cost?"

"Lemme worry bout it.."

"Sure, okay, sweet." Felix gave an enthusiastic smile because that sounded good to him, he was glad Vic was doing something different to get out of the dark funk he'd been in lately. And really, even if they did just end up doing a slug run, they'd be making toasts and flirting with the waitresses back at the cantina just a few hours from now, letting today fade into the next. So all good still.

The sound of shouting brought him back. An abscess of open space ringed a bedraggled woman at the tent's entrance.

"Oohs, flya alert," Vic said as they drew near. The flyer stomped about, protesting.

"*MERIT, LOGIC, FREEDOM, PEACE*! When will all the troubles cease!

MERIT, LOGIC, FREEDOM, PEACE, when will all the

troubles *cease*?

THESE, THE PRINCIPLES OF OUR FOUNDERS HAVE BEEN FORGOTTEN!

You there! You there! The time is come, are you prepared?

For twelve score and four years, the whole of time! You there! What have you done?

Whose city is this that is EATING ITS CHILDREN!

SWALLOWING ITS YOUNG!

And what have you done? The children, don't you hear!

No one listens, to the children, WHERE will they go? You there!

Where do they go? We must ask. We must demand. THEY know!

THEY know, you bet THEY do in their towers,

Even as they prowl the streets and dangle from the eaves.

THEY watch all of us and know, you know and you know—you there!

Do you believe that the terror of change will come? Do you know it believes in you?

Do you hear me? Do you believe what the city is telling you! *MERIT, LOGIC, FREEDOM, PEACE—*"

Her dress was well on its way to rags, smeared and ripped. A wood sandwich board with an illegible manifesto scrawled in hundreds of tiny red letters dangled over her neck. She roved back and forth, thrusting a haggard mass of handbills at anyone she could get close enough to.

By unanimous decision, all the passing strangers pretended the woman didn't exist. Some put up a hand as they passed to blot her from their vision, but most walked straight by, letting her tirade bounce off their ears, entry denied.

"Huh, haven't heard the "eating the children" one before, that's creative." Felix cracked, glancing back as the crossed the threshold of the big tent over the plaza.

"Bad way ta go, gettin et. Nuffin ever ets ye in juss one bite. Ye git chewed up first, bit atta time." Vic said.

"*Scuse me!*" a city voice called behind them.

Felix turned as a reflex, the flyer woman was following them. He made eye contact with a pocked and wind-worn face, polished to a sunburnt shine. That wasn't a Storm symptom, though the crazed pupils were. It was just what happened when you had no home, living under the constant elements of the city. Still, she wasn't an old woman as she appeared at first. Under the grime and the piercing stare was a young-ish face, they could have been the same class in grade school. She was tugging on his sleeve, addressing him.

"Ay, ay, wha'gwan!"

Felix slowed and gave a charitable wave.

"Wha'gwan." He greeted her back.

"Ay! Yer a Wizard, right?"

"What makes you say that?"

"*Felix*letsgobruv—"

She raised her eyebrows like it was obvious.

"Felix. Felicitiares? Course. Im really out here born in the LC, Logic Causeway, yah mean? Ye ent from a Causeway with a name like *Felicitiares.* Thatsa college-boy-wizard-type name, innit?"

"Yeah, but how did you know before he said my name?"

"Simp, ya Wizards walk with ya hands in they pockets, like there ent nuff to worry bout out here. So—"

This was ironic, considering the source's behavior, but apart from the unnerving look in her eye the woman didn't seem too far 'Touched when she wasn't proselytizing. She could turn it on and off. She must not have been struck directly. He felt the crowd watch them talking. Vic was fidgeting next to him, deciding whether to just walk away.

"Hey..." Felix said, trying to affect kindness, and not glance around— "You should probably get going. Take a walk to a different neighborhood. Try to find somewhere to sleep or go inside for a while. You look like you need a break—"

"Nope, nope, nope, nope!" She was already waving her head back and forth, talking over him. She spread her arms in a wide V, indicating all of existence. "Not tired. Can't be. All of this is ending soon, if we don't act. Lots of work. It's going to be okay though, I know what to do—just need your help, get some Wizard face-time. Someone high up. I have *ideas*, right? Look, I arranged it in a logical-type proof, like the Wizards do. Solvo One." She pointed meaningfully at the first bullet point of her sign.

"Kay, I'm going." Vic said, feinting away with his body.

"Wait just a second."

"Bruv!"

The flyer-lady bulled on, not keen to lose her audience, leaving no space between words for breath.

"*SINCE* the DISCOVERY OF HEAVEN, *TWELVE SCORE AND FOUR YEARS AGO,* and the signing of the DEMARCATION TREATY of YEAR TWENTY with the ROYAL ALIEN BLOOD EMPIRE,

which set the City of Heaven's as the edge of the lake and no further,

the city's population has grown faster than THE FOUNDERS could have ever intended,

AS YOU MUST AGREE."

"Sure, I mean—"

"SOLVO TWO— As even *SIMPS* can see:

by the *BROWNOUTS, FOOD PANICS, LAST SEASON'S AT-TEMPTED COUP, ETCETERA,*

there is no *MATHEMATICAL POSSIBILITY*

of the city's still-growing population being supported within its borders."

"Right, everyone knows that. Hey, we gotta—"

"Wait! No, don't leave, I'll skip to the good part. Please listen! Here, here— SOLVO EIGHTEEN!

With the ongoing insta*BILITY*—" she said, finally finding her level, "The Expansion of the *CIVIC WORKER POLICY,*

the disconnect of *THE ACADEMOCRACY* from its people,

the growing *COST of LIVING,*

and the unwillingness of ***DECEPTIVE ZURI LEADERSHIP*** in the city

to reign in their people's *RAPING, STREET MURDER, and CHEM PEDDLING,*

there *is NO CHOICE* for us but to *RECLAIM THE IL-LEGALLY OCCUPIED SOUTH BANK,*

RETAKING by ANY MEANS, THAT WHICH IS OURS BY RIGHT, AND HERITAGE!!"

As a final flourish she thrust a handbill into Felix's hand. He looked down at the stamped image— the silhouette of a dreadlocked head, with large drops of blood falling from the bottom, and a badly-proportioned axe above.

GOOLI GO HOME, it read.

The crowd, more than half Zuri, was really listening to them now. He dropped the paper like it was on fire, backing up, raising his hands. Vic tugged him away, and he proffered the woman a weak no thank you, but it didn't matter— she had gotten herself so worked up she had forgotten about them, stomping back into her one-person protest.

III

They tried to distance themselves as quickly as possible, under the Zuris' glaring scrutiny. With the WSWN in full effect none of the tribesmen were going to take a chance with the law by laying a hand on her, even if she was Stormtouched, but Felix could feel their caged anger seething across the courtyard.

"Ye wanna go agree wiff the crazy racist Stormtouched lady summore, blud?" Vic asked in a hiss as they sped.

"Sorry, I didn't know! They aren't all anti-Zuri. I was just trying to get her to go before—"

"Ye never know wiff em, dats why ye dont *talk* to em."

"Just trying to be— nevermind." He knew what his friend would say.

"Yeh yeh. Forget it, s'over. Now. Help me find someone who looks like dey know big birds."

"Birds?"

"Yes, bruv. Beeg birds."

"Am I supposed to know what that means? You're going to have to be more specific."

"The shovelbills! Remember? Stripey feddahs, tallah den you, travels in gangs en shite, big fookin beaks, kind'll stab ye eye out?"

"Right, right, for the feathers, I remember."

"Yeh. En the beaks en feet sell too, plus the livah." Vic whispered. "Dont mattah, well just plunk it at all down wiff the Rangers Guild. Prices up all round. The labs buyin erryting like mad. Nuffin but dosh in the forest bruv right now, waaay bettah den fookin ink slugs."

"And ay, I tink I clocked someting no one knows. Cummon— Lets find someone who ent cost a milli."

"I thought we were good on money?"

"Yeh yeh, but dese mans hit ye ovah the head onna contract if ye not careful. We juss wanna one-en-done-juss-today-type ting."

"No contract, does birds."

"Ye clocked it."

They walked into the tent away from everyone who had seen what happened, and looked around. The canopied square was full of jostling bravados, young Zuri hiring themselves out as guides, displaying themselves for the hunting parties that came, who swept their gaze over the lot without commitment.

The guides were garbed out somewhere between tribal warrior and street ruffian. The more fur, or scales, or teeth round the neck the newer in town they were. The recent arrivals were marked in manner as well: they stood around, planted unblinking next to their weapons, no idea how to market themselves.

Then there were those that had lost the feathers and copped a visored polyplax helmet, abandoned the braided belt for a bandolier, strapped with vials of healing potions, investing in the gear that made them career mercenaries, motivated once a few successful contracts had given them a taste of what loose cash could buy you in Heaven.

These were the market leaders of the Aerohub day labor pool. In addition to upgrading their gear, they had developed a basic notion of advertising. The most assimilated of the warriors had camped themselves out and picketed the area with banners and flags, coated with pictographs of various beasts, numbers and rates scrawled next to them, lots of fine print like Vic warned. They formed little mafias that blocked the sidewalk and let the most fluent of the pack barter for them in choppy pidgin, leaving the solo arrivals to find space wherever they could in the periphery, to figure it out for themselves.

Felix shook his head to turn his brain on, and actually engaged his eyes on the scene around him. The stalls in the tented plaza formed a square within a square for you to walk around, the inner and outer ring flush with the day's selection.

"Kay bruv, who looks like a good bounty huntah?"

"Well, technically, we're the bounty hunters, so I think we're hunting for a mercenary to assist our bounty hunting."

"Ye know wot I mean."

They side-eyed the hawkers trying to reel them, trying to learn something useful without obligating themselves. They walked down one side, sussing prices and specialties while avoiding eye contact with the pushier man-peddlers.

"All dese mooks look like idiotes, posers, thief tings." Vic said of the assembled sellers they were passing, frowning at the prices.

"We could try the solos over there, they're probably cheaper?"

"Cuz dats all the rejects who cant hack it and virgins who never done dis."

But they walked that way anyway.

Midway along the wall of unstalled guides-for-rent, there was a figure reclined, back against one of the wooden pillars rigging up the tent, ass on a barrel, head tilted back with a hood that fell past his nose, so they couldn't see if he was watching or not. He was a picture of casual repose in a morass of posture and selling, no gaudy banner or hype-man. His only concession to branding himself was a rectangular sign propped up in front of him: KILLETH I EVERY-THING – NO CONTRACT NEEDED. They couldn't see his face between the hood and the dreadlocks dangling out of it, but there was a different energy that stood him out from the rest.

"How 'bout him? Lotta feather tats. Probably knows birds." Felix said.

"Mebbe."

They approached.

"Ay, hi, wha'gwan, Onga-longa!" Vic said, taking the lead.

The tribesman tilted his head up slightly and pulled the dreads out of his face. A stern set of dark brown eyes looked past a large, angular nose, and pronounced the word right in a deep voice.

"Olingolo go."

"Eh, close. Everyting, innit?" Vic said, eyeing the sign.

"So far, yes."

"Ha. Kay. So— shovelbills. Ye *know* bout dem, bruv?"

"Mmhmm." He grunted back.

"Dats a yes? Shovelbills? Big bird-type ting?"

"Mhmm. With large talons. Liketh to eat eyeballs. Feathers, stripedy."

"Clocked it, kay, wass ya rate den?"

"Five hundo."

"Wot? For a day? Blud, ye serious?"

"Art thou?" he asked, unblinking.

"*Pfft.* The most! Sorry, thought ye was someone who wanted to work today."

"I doth. But for ones with five hundo for me. Can killeth

everything. No contract. Readeth sign."

"Blud, git real. No one out here chargin more'n a hundo or two." He squinted at the guy, not a pretty sight. "How old are ye even? Have ye evah even done dis evah?"

"Yeah, you think you're worth five of those guys?" Felix said, pointing at a booth across the way. At it, a contingent of Midnight Leopard Boys (according to their banner) sparred, shadow-boxed, and arm-wrestled. They dripped in full body leopard tats, with head gear and shoulder pads to match. Their barker, a short fellow, zipped his head towards Felix, sensing the interest. Felix shoved his gaze back to the conversation, hopefully before it was too late.

"They haveth contract."

"Bruv, chill, I got dis— yeh tho, why shouldnt we rent anyadese man dem over there instead?"

"Thou should. Thou can payeth me not."

"Eh, slow down, who said dat? Blud, we just talkin, innit. okay, forreal— wots yer low?"

"Five hundo."

"Cummon! I give ye two. Juss for the day. Ye cant be gettin much work like dis."

"I doth not need much work like this."

"This guy really knows how to slut." Felix said.

"*Bruv, shut it, I got dis*— so, wot, you got like a, a doshback-guarantee-type ting if we dont catch nuffin, or wot?"

The feather-woven teen ruffian gave them a haughty laugh and sneered. "Goeth to them. The contract-men. They will helpeth you for your little bank."

Vic sizzled, and pinched his temples. Felix tried to lighten the air.

"Hey, it's no worries man! It's cool. Sorry, if you don't mind me asking, what tribe are you from? I don't recognize those marks, and I always like to ask."

"White Crow."

"Oh! That's interesting, I never learned about that one. Is it a smaller tribe? Is your homesite very far?"

"Not far."

"Okay okay okay okay okay okay okay." Vic said, waving away their side-conversation with a brusque hand, "Ye dont havva contract."

"As I say."

"Alright... all yer own gear? Ye got a chute?"

"Here." He patted a bundle next to him.

"Okay, super super! Signeth here boss, good picks!" Felix felt a poke in his back and a high pitched voice.

He turned and saw a wall of purple.

"'Five of these guys! You sayeth, delivereth we! My best Leopard boys, for your hunting trip today!"

The barker, a shorter fellow with big silver gems studded into his leopard head's sockets, pressed a clipboard into Felix's solar plexus. The dinky man looked a little bigger with his five muscled friends behind him.

"Yup, no money down. First trip free, good choice, super stuff boss. Sign!" A sinking feeling hit Felix. He looked at the guy with the crow tats, who just shrugged, still seated.

"Err, hey, wait, we were talking to someone already here—"

"Pah, the suckling, has no crew? Friend, looketh. Purple Leopards stand here and taketh his business all the day, cuz better we be. You look smart, a Wizard right?"

"Dont sign." Vic said. "Ay. Ye and yer guys can all *git* with it, no one hired ya idyots."

"Sure, sure boss! No problems. Incurreth you a cancellation fee tho, how payeth thee?"

"I don't, cuz Im not stupid."

25

"Hey, big agree here. Keepeth it one hundo. Knoweth I *you* the smart one, and knoweth you this the best deal. No money down today, means more for you."

"Listen, please, this is a misunderstanding—" Felix said.

"We worketh on credit, no moneys down, comes with free health potion, free Aero pass, first time, *super* good deal. Better than dis guy, on the realeth real…"

He just kept going. All of the promotional language swam into Vic, and some didn't come back out. Felix could see his friend moving mental abacus beads around.

Vic was about to say let me read this, when someone screamed up front by the street. A mammal-noise. It crimped the hairs on the back of Felix's neck, and he turned with everyone else. The noise repeated in tormented bursts. Everyone was coming out of their booths, moving to the middle of the square to stand on toes for a glimpse.

"No, *HAAAAAAALP!*"

The cry morphed into words, piercing over the heightened hush of the watching crowd.

The black wagon was blasted up onto the curb. Its suicide doors hung open like mechanical labia. Out of it, a pair of Rangers walked. Three-color armbands, black overcoats— unlike Vic, a Jungle Ranger, this was a City Corps Response team. The City arm of the Rangers Guild was the only group the Wizards paid to employ violence to get things done, the rest of the City had to do it for free. They were the ones who arrived when streets needed to be kept safe from rioters, saboteurs, looters, madmen, kidnappers, Homesteader robbers, blatant pimps and chem pushers, escaped Civic Workers, grifters, drifters, vagrants, graffitists, the unlawfully assembled, anarchists, flyers, child predators, and the homeless. Both carried a silver device slid over their right wrist, one part tight-fitting glove and one part halo, encircling their hand around the thumbk-nuckle. The strapshot was a marvel in crowd control tech. It was sensitive to pressure and responded to hand gestures fluidly, so effective at its job it was unlawful for citizens to possess. Anyone could have one used on them though.

"They've got *straps*," Felix murmured.

"Dey all do now bruv, wake up. Prolly they just keep em on Net mode for her, too bad, blud. She a crazy racist ting."

"No! *Do you see?* HAAALP!" The Stormtouched woman cried, backing into the tent plaza. The thin crowd near the front moved out of the way of the black-clad lawmen. They approached her with slow, wide stance. Everyone was silent.

One of the Corps beckoned to her with a cupped hand. She darted backwards, and cried in anguish. The front of the crowd didn't yield. Someone pushed her back towards them with a grunt. She stumbled, tripping on her sign-board, almost fell.

They kept closing. Both lifted their arms, thumbs jab-bing out. As their digits extended, the silver halo filament circling the strapshots made a click and a flash, and two white webs of plasma burst out to ensnare her.

She went flat out—the first plasma net went low and missed, scrambling with energy on the pavement as it faded inert. The second one hit her, but wrapped mostly the signboard. She clawed it off her neck and staggered up, scampering on bleeding knees scraped to tatters and scrambled right fast, to the wall. The men saw where she was going and dashed toward, as she grabbed at the rope line that tied down one side of the canopy tent.

Hauling herself up, she used the rope and the pole and the brick wall to brace herself but there was nowhere to go. In a second she had treed herself, but couldn't get out of reach of the Corps, who came behind her and yanked at her legs and hips, breaking her hold, digit by slipping digit, sending her crashing back down to the pavers.

Then it was over. Her last sounds clipped off as the black bag slipped over her face. The second Ranger made a show of flipping her over, and binding her wrists and ankles with a pack of cable ties at his waist. The first walked and collected her sign, before they tossed both through the van's waiting hole. It clapped shut.

Some people clapped a little. Others just went back to work with a quick saying or jibe. The noise rose back to normal levels. Felix mopped the cold sweat from his face, and sucked in breath, trying to slow his heart rate and unsee all of that.

"Finally," Vic said, sympathetic. "Fore she hurt somebody, or got stomped out. S'good. She gonna git the help she needs now."

"Yeah." Felix managed to say, from the back of the library of dark memories in which he now found himself. He knew what kind of help was waiting for her at the Colleges, in the labs. His old work study job. *Don't think about it*, he told himself. He just focused on those words. *Don't think about it. Act normal. Stop shaking. Open your eyes.*

An expletive from Vic made it easier. His friend was agog. Felix now became aware that all of the Leopard Boys were on the ground. Sometime in the commotion they had all six of them decided to take a lie down. A trickle of blood was sliding out of more than one of their hidden noses. The casual Zuri with the feather tats was standing up now, cracking his knuckles and looking at them, face *blasé*.

None of the crowd or other Leopard Boys by the tent had registered it yet, but they were starting to.

"Oh, fook—go, bruv, go, we ent need no guide, quick, fore the uddahs look—"

Felix obliged. They hurried back towards the front to leave, but found more to see. A bunch of guys were clustered in the front right corner, shouting at each other and pointing up.

The tent was not designed to be ascended. Where the woman had climbed, a rope had pulled out of tautness, and this little change had put enough slack in a corner that the constant rain was beginning to pool. This was putting a growing sac of rainwater directly above their collective heads. It seemed simple to just tighten the slack, but all of the braided lines securing the canvas to the poles were linked together, so the time it would take to readjust one section would allow just as much rain to accumulate on its neighbors. To truly fix it, you'd have to clear everyone out, and re-erect it from scratch. That was impossible obviously— not enough time, so there *had* to be some way to fix this one problem in isolation, or what a major design flaw it would be. No one was agreeing on it though, or getting a cogent plan together. Meanwhile, the weight of the water was building, and putting more strain on the poles and other ropes, minute over minute.

Felix sussed the building tension on the lines: outlook not good. Some precocious individuals around started to pack up their things, or just stood and left, noting what was about to happen.

"Hey, this whole thing is about to come down," Felix said, in a detached, sing-song way, pointing at one particular strand of rope coiling and pulling thin. Vic looked up and came to the same conclusion.

"*Oosh*— no good! Wottarye doin bruv, juss wotchin it— bail!" he said, loud enough the people around them heard and looked up. These folks aw they were already behind the getting out of dodge power curve, and chaos bred. It was a stampede by the time they made it to the threshold, people shoving one another to escape.

SNAP. The thin line broke. A half-ton of water went into freefall for a few feet, before being caught by what tension was left, doubling the strain placed on the remaining supports. This paradigm lasted for a few seconds, until the cumulative weight became too much for one of the middle poles.

It didn't split and flatten down the middle all of a sudden like Felix anticipated. It yawed to the heavy side like a capsizing boat, ripping all of the other lines still attached from their eyelets, so that the light side collapsed first, from the edges. The water, with no counterbalance, crushed down to the ground, splintering the rigged-up posts, and finally deposited its reserve onto the square, smashing and flooding everyone and thing in it. Mortal cries emerged from the back of the wreckage.

The two friends saw all of this in steals over their shoulder, running away, still looking out for purple leopard cloaks following them.

Felix's heart was hammering. He reached into his pocket and pulled out his flask. He tilted it and sucked as they pushed through the crowd, watching Vic's back ahead of him.

He knew it was early. He knew he shouldn't. He needed it still. The WSWN was in full effect.

It's not as bad as what's about to happen to that woman, a deep-down voice said.

He drank some more.

Don't think about it.

IV

Felix and Vic fled back around the block and into the Aerohub proper. Felix tucked the flask away, and fished a mint out of his pocket to cover his breath. His head was floating nicely now, memories once again distant. They came to the rear of the queues, leading to the different terminal gates, and were soon bricked in by more arriving behind them. Vic pulled them into a line slowly parading beneath a roloboard, ZORTELL CREVASSE + SNAKEPIN DIP + ZUMELIN'S LAKE picked out in its flipdown letters. As they came to a stop and made a quick final check for any vengeful Leopards, Felix noticed that the Zuri with the feather tattoos had followed, standing right next to them in silence, looking straight ahead.

"Wot a shiteshow! A*ha!*" Vic shook off the excess energy. He gave Felix a perilous grin, riding the adrenaline high like the grime-lifed Causeway kid he was. He bounced a few times and slapped their new Zuri friend on the arm.

"Ayy! You dosed dem mooks bruv! Whatcha do em with!?"

"My hands."

"Bruv! How!?"

The young one shrugged. "By hitting. In the right spots. I knoweth the right spots." He jammed two fingers at his clavicle, and at a bone on his jaw, demonstrating. "And I haveth hate for them."

"Wot, dem purple boys?"

"All like them. The city tribes. The meat-men. The self-sellers. I am a real one. They fake."

"Right, cuz its diffrent den wot yer doin out here, cuz..."

"Wait—" Felix blurted. "Real ones...you're Zuri Orthodox! Well, I guess you wouldn't call yourself that, it's an externally-ascribed moniker."

Both of them looked at him blankly, and he realized he was talking like a full-blown Wizard student.

"I mean, there are some Zuri who have come to live like city people, and then there are ones who only follow the old ways of living, like you."

"Yes." He said. "I liketh to hit the first kind."

"Wots the diff, ye can hunt a bluddy shovelbill yeh?"

"Well, there are a lot of differences, for instance—" Felix called up the memories of a Zuri anthropology class he had taken years ago.

"Yes." The newcomer continued to Vic as if Felix hadn't spoken.

"Great. Guess yer with us den."

The dread-headed one scratched his tattooed neck. "Almost." he said.

"Ah. Right." Vic turned away and hunched over for a bit, and re-faced them with three bills, two aqua-green and one pink, an even two hundo fitty. The bills were murky with stains, overlaying the diorama of civic imagery printed on the fabric strips— ideal views of the Colleges overlooking the Causeways, the city pictured as it was just after the Settlement, framed by scrolled banners decrying the three ideals. He held them out, their new friend did not reach.

"But this is *not* five hundo."

"No, its half blud, en dats genrous. Ye can git the rest tonight when were back, or wheneva we hit a catch. Take it or leave it, blud."

The warrior's eyes wrinkled, before he placed a flat hand out. Felix's best bruv winced as his money vanished into the recesses of a hooded cloth garm. Felix suspected Vic may have been trying to drive the guide away with a lowball, but ended up getting a payment plan instead.

The newest member of their crew issued a half-satisfied grunt. "What doth I call you?"

"Call me Veek bruv. Dis mook is Felix, my backup. He from the Colleges, the Pyramids, the big shiny buildings, ye understand what I'm sayin? Good. Wizard ting, now hes slummin it with me, we live on Merit," Vic said, referring to the housing projects on Merit Causeway, not a personal philosophy. "En you?"

"For cityboys—Jim-mee." He baritoned.

"Jimmy, sure. Works for me."

Another grunt. The barbarian pointed at Felix with his forehead, talking to Vic—

"So he is Wizard? He does the brain Magic?"

"Nah, nah. He dropped out, s'okay. He ent do it nomore."

"But be he a good hunter? Because I have workethed for Wizards."

"Dude, Jimmy? I'm right here, you can talk to me too. I know how to hunt, we've done this a dozen times."

Jimmy paused.

"What?" Felix said, to both of them. The barbarian gave him a rank twitch of his nostrils and turned to Vic.

"He drinketh the city poison. This hour, drinketh he. Can smell. This, in jungle, is very bad. When drinketh the city poison, men get slow, heareth things not, is dangerous. Drinkers watcheth not the backs of others."

Felix suppressed a wily hiccup, and burned a little at another Look from Vic. He egged on a smile.

"Hey, I'm fine! Come on, it's my day off. I'm fine, definitely by the time we jump. I'm here, I'm serious, no worries."

Jimmy, unimpressed, continued to speak to Vic.

"For why did you hireth him?"

"He ent gettin paid, hes my roommate. Free. Hes an *idyot*, but worth it. Mosta the time. Now cummon."

Jimmy made a very professional noise. Vic didn't like something about this and hardened a little.

"I said cummon blud. Git ovah it, play nice. S'be fine. I ent hire ye as a moral compass, yer here to murda wildlife with us, innit?"

During this convo, they had moved up the line and through the turnbuckle and maneuvered through the packs of other jungle-bound travelers. They pushed up into one of the raised terminals to buy a ticket from an Aeromobile line operator. This choice brooked no argument. Felix and Vic were die-hard Choppers Unlimited loyalists.

Other airlines coddled their passengers— secured them in padded seats, bribed them with complementary protein snacks, free health potions and other meaningless swag. These operators invested in petty comforts for their fleets, like shock absorbers and seat belts. Choppers Unlimited, LLC gave no truck to such "compete-on-quality" touches. A ride in a CU rig was like being thrown through the air in a perforated metal bucket. Their customers were on average more knowledgeable about the absolute minimums of Aero maintenance and cleaning required by law, because of the CU corporate family's daily example.

Working class para-commuters like Vic swore by the brand. Felix and other social derelicts enjoyed the leeway to drink and smoke aboard without peer judgement.

Choppers was also the smallest Aero-enterprise, the

only one that hadn't been conglomerated or ventrilo-
quized by the larger companies, a hold-out in the prevail-
ing industry winds. Which was crazy, Aeromobiles hadn't
even been a thing until twenty seasons agoish.

It had taken two hundred years for Heaven to reinvent
flight technology, the wreckage of Arks recycled long ago,
useless without the Old Continent fuel anyway. Felix re-
membered watching the first modern flightcraft he ever
saw as a kid, looking out through the shaded blue window
of Farseilles College, where his father was posted before
being ascended to his position in the Edifice.

He and his sister had commentated the airship's bum-
bling flight, laughing and rooting it on as it rose up almost
level with their penthouse on the twenty eighth level. It
crashed a minute or so later, one rotor failing with a chunk,
sending the mechanical carapace spilling down into the
lake with a distant splash. That happened a lot, in the early
months. After Lordon and Vapour, two Wizards-gone-pri-
vate-sector, finally cracked the brainlock on sustained
flight by combining the latest applications in streamlin-
ing, rotor tech, and battery magic, the island had become
a battlefield of tinkerers and contraptionists racing their
prototypes into the sky, littering the lake with attempts.
Several dozen companies ended up with working models,
originally operating off of floating runways anchored in
the lake, before several coastal neighborhoods were rearranged to create the Aerohub.

They began offering parachute flights to outbound Rangers, the whole dosh-making point of it all, injecting the
city's hunters directly into the jungle's heart and cutting
out days of overland travel out through the city's gates at
the far end of the Causeway bridges. Within a few weeks of
the tech going public, the range of Heavenly exploration

expanded by hundreds of kilometers.

A good half of the original operators were lost in the next two years; couldn't hack the ensuing regulatory cycles that hounded the inventions. The tech had proliferated far faster than the Wizards had anticipated and the racket disturbed the neighbors. The Zuri tribes now had men raining like strange fruit into untouched regions. This led to a new wave of bloody clashes in the jungle and more tension between the City and the tribes since the sanguine seasons that led to the original Demarcation Treaty, which set Heaven's border at the Lake's shore and no further. Hunting, travel, and trade were all provisioned for in the trade, but this new skyborne pipeline was seen as beyond the pale.

Limitations came down hard and knocked many Aero companies out of the sky overnight, in order to maintain the goodwill that allowed Heaven to remain on the map. More were lost in the labyrinth of permits and safety specs that led unerringly to more fees at every turn. Of those who made it through to the modern Aeromobile paradigm, a select few managed to find the favor of the Wizards doing the regulating. These groups turned their advantage into alphahood.

That was a decade or so back. After the crisis subsided, none of the rules or laws had been updated since but the field had narrowed, as the strongest competitors bankrupted and bought out any industry mates who flagged into a vulnerable position. The number of different Aerolines running active flights had absorbed down to ten, and then to seven last dry season, after three company's fleets were ransacked past salvation by crowds (or competitor-paid crisis actors, who knew?) during the solarcell brownouts. When the lights came back on, the city's growing population found itself with less options to fly with than ever.

There was a terminal on either side of the AeroHub. You had to find the code for the dropsite you wanted to get on with the ticking roloboards on the walls, then find a flight number going there. You'd then turn around and find this flight number in real life, emblazoned in fat figures the hulls of the Aeros to give even the most illiterate customer no doubt. The last part was to get on one and buy a ticket before it hermetically sealed itself and blistered off the business end of the launch rail.

The Aeros were all styled and colored by brand, but followed the same base schematic— A beetly hull with a chunky cockpit for a head, a riveted metal thorax big enough to hold 20ish chute jumpers in a go. A four-blade rotor lay slicked back on the roof and the wings were stood up parallel with the body of the beast, in resting position. Every minute and fifteen seconds a bell blared and a hidden crankshaft ratcheted the whole procession forward, kicking the front spot out to do its thing.

They noted a strange air as soon as they stepped in, and the board confirmed it. Choppers Unlimited was gone. There were no brushed silver Aeros (CU never wasted customer money on paint) and no gray glyphs on the board. It seemed the ineffable had happened. The stalwart of the Aerohub, the last dissenting alternative to the overpriced and shiny had finally succumbed. This threw Vic into a brief conniption, as he calculated how much the average cost of flying had just increased, out loud, for several minutes.

V

They found themselves on a shuttle run by *iPhly*, a disgustingly well-kept Aero with beveled off-white everything. Vic forked over an unsympathetic premium to the ticket-taker, she wore a different Causeway's tattoos and the two handled the transaction with mutual contempt. The passenger hull was lined with seats that flipped down from the wall. Vic kept grumbling as they stowed their things and readied their compressed parachute vests.

"Fook bruv, I cant *believe* dat! Fitty a ticket— the costa doin anyting in the jungle just jumped. Erryone who chutes for work gonna feel it."

The amount they had spent this morning seemed very high to Felix. He did the math against their reserve for the month, but realized that couldn't be right, so he pushed the thought away.

"Well, are you surprised?" he said instead. "It was inevitable."

"I remember when twenny was high—"

"The cost of everything in this city is only going one way." Felix shrugged and sighed.

Vic's good eye rolled. "Yeh yeh, well. Ent dat bad. Dont git all depressed with me. Yer startin to sound like dat flya lady back there, all dat kinda talk, drop it. Weve got shite to do today."

"Sorry, it's not like I made it up— if it's depressing, it's because it's true, it's reality. Anyone with their eyes open and half a brain can tell that things are bad and getting worse. It doesn't take a Wizard to see that. Heaven is just doomed."

"Then fook Heaven bruv! No, Im *serious* bruv. focus on you. All ye can do is make yer shite bettah. Figga out which way *yer* goin, not the fookin city. Cant do nuffin bout dat. Lifes always been hard, lowah Heaven's always been like this. Ye cant fight gainst it."

"That's what they want us to believe." Felix said, in dark vagary. "Speaking of which, where are we going today, if we're not going to the slug cliffs?"

"Alright, sure. Let's do this. Jimmy, you hears me?" Vic fished a map out of his backpack. The young barbarian had gone glaring off into space again, and turned back to them with a blink.

The map was greasy with thumbprints and wax smudges. Diamond holes had torn into the intersecting creases from a thousand foldings. He flapped it open, and stuck a finger at an X crissed into the map with a red crayon mark.

"Alright. So. We drop in here. S'the same dropsite we hit like normal, only today, were not goin up the trail to the Crevasse, were goin around, past all the idyots tryna make a nut offa slugs, and keep going."

"To where?" Jimmy said, puzzled.

"Ill tell ya when were on the ground. Gotta good spot."

"Why shovelbills?" Felix said.

"Shh!" Vic hissed and jerked his head around the Aero, at the other teams and solos hanging around, in their own conversations.

"Dont say nuffin like dat bruv— Dis ting fulla dimlits who would *keel* for wott I found out."

"This land place," Jimmy said, pointing to the Crevasse,

shaking his head. "Hath no birds. Too close to river. And too early. Only breed in dry season. Wanteth you the big birds? We go here. Here. Or here." He said, pointing around the map. "In three more moons when season turn. On different Aero. Not here."

"Ay!" Vic said, shutting the map. "Wot I juss say? Keep ye voice down round all dese hungry muthas. Yer gonna see when we git there. Juss be ready to hunt. I know wot Im talkin bout."

"How?" Felix said.

"I fookin did research, innit? One of us actually prepares for dese trips." Vic snapped.

"Alright, alright— and no slugs at all today."

"Are ye deaf, mate? I already said dat."

"Just making sure that's the plan."

"Yes! Fook blud."

"It's whatever man, I'm just here to help."

"This land-place," Jimmy said again, "Is also big place for the Storm." He left the word hanging, an implied threat on its own.

"Oh, don't worry about that!" Felix said. "I got us there." He whipped something palm-sized out of his vest. The tawny wood box had grooves to fit your hand, and a little cover that flipped smooth on hinges to show three circular dials with free spinning arrows. He scrutinized where each arrow pointed on its tiny wheel.

"*Feeelix.*" Vic pushed Felix's hand down into his lap, covering the device.

"Put it away, dese tings is crawlin with thieves!" he whispered close.

"Man, relax." Felix said, jerking away. "Why are you so tense?"

"Cuz neitha of ye know how to act on an Aero, s'why. Im

tryna be proffesh out here."

The Aero was approaching the end of the rail. In a few minutes a flow of solar magic running through the rail would touch to a contact plate on the undercarriage, allowing the technical Wizardry built into the machine's wings and rotors to animate. The thaumatic wave flowed into the guts of the rig until every ungrounded piece quivered with kinetic overclock. Touching a live Aero sent enough force into your bloodstream to stop the hearts of your family members three generations in either direction, and was generally considered a bad idea. The machines needed enough juice to loop out over the jungle and make it back to the Hub— there were no landing yards in the jungle, only drop zones and crash sites. Each pilot only got one shot, no kidding, so once an Aero had charged enough to be lethal, the doors were sealed, you were in or out.

"I don't have to come," Felix said. "I don't want to mess up your plans." A montage of saloons with daytime happy hours rolled through his mind.

"Oh, yer comin. Dis racket dont have refunds."

That settled, they settled in. Felix turned away from his friend and leaned his head on the porthole window to try to clear his mind in vain. He slipped his hand into his vest pocket to give the Storm-reader and his flask a securing squeeze. As they passed a striped pillar on the terminal, the ticket-taker girl yelled for seatbelts and engaged a multi-stage lever controlling the pneumatics. She came to stand right over Felix, who had ended up with the end seat. He watched the grooved door close itself and closed his eyes.

The vibration running through the wall into his head gradually grew until his temple was knocking on the rubber gasket. When the quaking reached the level where Felix was sure it the Aero was about to detonate it took a vomiting lurch forward, and the shutters separating the battered magic from its mechanical terminus swung open. His stomach jumped as the triplet rotors sprung up to full speed in a mighty rev, and the rest of him presumed to follow. When he opened them, they were shooting upward into the sky and leaving lower Heaven.

On their way up they passed through the Drone Belt strata. The hull of the ship *whoomped* as something the size of a cat caromed off of it. A new conceptual arrival, the courier drones had proliferated as fast as the r-strategists they mimicked. It seemed as soon as the first prototype was released, a swarm of its ten thousand closest friends had trailed, and almost overnight the way town business was done had changed. Wizards loved them! It meant they could trade information between College buildings even faster and go outside less. As always, they frantically dashed out a few regulations in the spirit of public safety, fearful of drones crashing their scissory little rotors into windows, children, etc, anticipating the potential injuries to be avoided. Hence the Drone Belt, it was the lowest legal altitude they could fly at. This was fine with the operators as well, considering not everyone was happy with these unmanned deliverers, prime sabotage targets. Nothing was more satisfying than to swipe a low-flying drone out of the air, especially if you were one of the twenty thousandish human couriers who had just been unmanned out of a job.

The roar of the rotors slacked off as they stopped climbing, smaller air traffic making way for them. Out the window, two person magekites plunged away on thermals, dipping and sailing beneath. Another Aero, returning to dock, leaned to avoid clipping a flame-colored luxury swingsail flying lackadaisically close. Felix saw the obscured outline of the pilot pounding his fist on the cockpit glass.

He gazed out the porthole at the varied, interplaying swarm of crafts, then looked down, to see the city-island and the lake growing smaller as the jungle swallowed it in his view.

"Hey, was that one of those new Storm-reader handhelds?"

He looked up. The ticket-taker girl was talking to him, fixing him with an expectant face. She was as fashion forward as her work clothes would allow. Indigo dye-streaked hair carved to her neck, fading up to an aggressive, cloudy pompadour. A pair of snakebite piercings clicked in her lower lip and two blue orbs gauged her earlobes, a lapis and a turquoise, two asymmetric moons, matching the full bleed of cosmetelogical warpaint accentuating her face. The virile male part of him saw a brimming chest and thick legs, bulging out where she leaned on the wall, he noted absently.

"Yeah. I work at Pagerock's. Got a discount."

"Hmm. Proud of yourself I bet." She jumped on his sentences with an overcaffeinated bite.

"I mean, not really as a point, there's—"

"You shouldn't be. Those things are just the latest tool to oppress the indigenous and poor people in this city."

"I don't think mine has that feature."

"Cute. They all do. You're lucky you have enough Wizard-privilege for that joke to be funny to you."

"I'm not a Wizard, I—"

"It was bad enough when no one could predict them. Now with your little readers, which no one I know, who actually works a job, could ever afford, getting turned into a flyer becomes even more of a poor person's problem."

"It's not the tech's fault. Someone could just as easily use it for the public good."

"But they won't."

"You're probably right." he said.

"Yeah, it's not your problem, why worry about it?"

"You know, I actually do have a job, like I just said, and I'd have gotten fired already talking the way you are to me."

"Whatever. They can can me, I don't care about this place. Also, what kind of Wizard has a job? You mean keeping your parents happy? *Bye.*"

"I'm not a Wizard. I dropped out a year ago. My father wishes I was dead."

"Oh, so sad. A failed Wizard is still a Wizard."

"I failed because I torched a classroom."

"On purpose?"

"Yes."

"Did anyone die?"

"Just my chances."

"Yeah, sounds dumb." She said, looking away with annoyance.

"So, does it actually work?" she said a second later, staring at her black nailtips.

"What?"

"The Storm-reader, duh. Does it work?"

"I thought you hated them."

"I hate that the people who actually need them can't afford them. Can I see it?"

Vic butted in, waving a hand at her. "Oo, sorry luv, nick one from someone else. Ye ent gettin ya claws on it. Step step now."

She gasped in offense and her lined eyebrows met on her forehead to form a rebuttal.

"She works here man, she's not a thief. We were just talking." said Felix.

"She from Freedom innit? Shes a thief bruv, I proms ye." He wiggled a finger past Felix's eye at the tattoos on the back of her hand.

"Fook off I said! Rangers ordahs."

She looked at Felix with dismay. "You're with an effin *Ranger*? Ew. Speaking of tools of oppression."

"Babe, Ill oppress ye so hard, ye gonna hafta git both yer brothers to stop blowin each other to come save ye."

The sides of her eyes pinched in discord. She stuck her little finger in the air and flicked, a universally understood sign of disrespect. "Go get raped. Merit creep." The girl huffed off the wall and walked to the other side of the bus. Jimmy didn't move an inch, as if he was painted into the chair.

"Dats right, keep it movin." Vic said as she walked past. He grinned his holey smile at Felix. Animosity between the children of the city's three Causeways (aspirationally named for the City's tripartite ideals) was alive and thriving. The rivalry twixt the gangs, businesses, public figures, Pit fighters and even average citizens raised on each of the island-city's three bridges was comedy fodder inside the halls of the Colleges where Felix was raised, and stereotyped as such:

- Merit dwellers (like Vic, and like Felix was trying to become) were drunk boorish goons, coarse as they were short-sighted.
- Logic folk were sheepish rule-followers, universally gullible and fatally dull.

- The Freedomers were inbreeders (hence Vic's over-ture) and backstabby connivers, irredeemable devi-ants.

There were sports teams, pulp theatre series, brightly-branded pride window flags blazoned to fuel the intra-hood hype. It was all a little weird to Felix, who didn't have any understanding of being proud of where you're from, but when you added up all the gang violence and develop-ment politicking, inter-Causeway business alliances, the tattoo language, and the general spirit of difference, he had to admit it was a very real factor to a lot of people.

Felix regarded his friend with his head to the side.

"Wot, ye tink ye was gonna link wiff her?" Vic scoffed.

"What, no!"

"Why not? Id do her. Not at my place, tho."

"Dude, why are you so para today? Ranger stuff?"

"Dat Storm-reada is juss espensive bruv, keep it put til we outta here." He crossed his arms.

The presence of good sense threatened Felix. He de-fended.

"I bought it with my money, didn't I? It's a free city, I can play with it if I want." Felix clowned. Vic's bony face dark-ened with a frown.

"Fine, be an idyot."

"I was just joking."

"Right."

"And she was just talking to me."

"Yeh. En ask yaself why."

Vic began to lean back all cool-like, but was rousted a moment later by a harsh throat clearing across the way. They broke their bubble to see an older man in full Jungle Ranger kit sitting there watching them. Disdain emitted from his nostrils at them. Felix laughed and Vic shushed him.

He was the real deal, the picture of Jungle Rangerhood — a muckskin vest dyed and darkened to a mottled array of jungle colors, with the gloves and boots to match. His cheeks and mouth were consumed by bristly beard, the wisps shocking to gray. Which meant he was an above average hunter at least, or pushing his luck. He sussed Vic like meat gone bad.

"Bad form, younger brother." He said, once they had all seen each other.

"Fo*ok, ah*, sorry, olda brotha, I dint—" Vic cut himself off and winced.

"You didn't what?" The older Ranger puffed up with outrage. "*See me there?* You are a Ranger, whether you are being watched or not. It is your job to stay *most* aware of your surroundings, so I'm not sure which is worse!"

"I know, sir."

"That is not how Rangers speak to ladies."

This earned an affronted ugh from the girl, who was still listening.

"Ye right, sir. Unacceptable. Wottan idyot I am Lemme fix it sir, post-fookin-haste. Ay! You!" He called down the tube. The girl looked away.

"Wots ye name, so I can do an apology?"

Vic stood when she didn't answer, and walked up close to read her name tag.

"Regina!" he said, dancing back out of her reach, half turning back to the older Ranger. "Regina, so, so sorry. It werent true. On behaffa the whole guild, City and Jungle Rangers both, I ent meant none of it. Rangers promise. Fahgive me." He returned and deposited himself into the seat without waiting for her response.

"There, sir." Vic said. Felix eyed the time until the drop, numbers winding down on a roloboard behind a wired cage. Less than five minutes. Would his friend make it without being stabbed with a makeup pencil or formally disciplined by a work superior? He waited to find out.

Vic's burst of manic energy pre-empted what the Ranger was about to do, which was make him apologize, so the older man was forced to regroup. He had two companions himself: a hefty-armed Zuri at his left, who paid no attention, flicking dust from his arm rest. On his right was another younger Ranger, closer in age to Vic and Felix, dark-complected with two brittle brown eyes, dancing between his boss and Vic, absorbing everything and saying nothing.

"Thank you, sir, I ppreciate ye correctin my conduct sir, it was not up to Ranger standards."

The man gave a minor version of the grunt that had started this whole thing.

"Identify yourself, young brother."

"Vic, sir, Jungle Corps, Rank 1, badge numbah 4689, freeknife, ready to Range."

"Hmm, well, you'll keep freeknifing for a while if you don't learn your etiquette. The clubs pay very close attention to reputation."

"Yessir! I agree sir. Dis is why I will prolly just continue to freeknife it actually, sir, it suits me."

This made the old guy laugh, he slapped his native companion's modern breastplate knowingly.

"Remember those days Tommy? New Rangers! Loba here was saying something similar earlier, how some of his friends think that. Like skipping from gig to gig is anyway to live. I remember how fun and exciting it was, watching the market, picking a mark, trying to get the next big catch, hunting something different every day. It is fun, grand fun when the days are full, but those empty ones get dire real quick. You'll learn."

"Sure, sir." Vic said, trying not to disagree, or remember a non-dire day in his short, poverty-filled life.

Felix tried to participate. "We were doing cliff slug runs for a while, for the glue factories. It was pretty good money too, but we can do better."

"Ah! Glue slugs at the Crevasse, that's a good start, part of how I came up myself. So you do understand how it works."

"No no, we ent runnin dat hustle nomore, it ent worf it. The Crevasse drop is juss close to where we need to go today. Sorry sir, but that just ent a good come up dese days. He ent know wot hes talkin bout." Vic said.

He laughed again. "You may think differently at some point, my boy! Listen to your cautious friend there. It's an opportunity to prove your worth, even if it's not glamorous. Consistency is just as key to ranging as flashy kills, over time. Your stats at the Guildhouse will show, you'll see what I mean. Give it a few seasons. You work up your reputation in the field, and once you've shown you can deliver what you say, on schedule, you will have everything you need for a club to recognize you when you apply. You'll come to appreciate it, and someday you'll be telling someone young like you the way it goes yourself. And then you can see some real perquisites— bounty shares, club equipment, the pension, if you make your twenty seasons. Though you probably can't even *hear* good advice at your age, none of those things mean much to you yet. It all just sounds like settling to you young ones, I'm sure."

"Sounds like a miracle," Vic said. "Musta been nice, bein in the game twenny years ago, when dat would actually work."

Felix snorted, he loved watching Vic run after his own mouth.

The bristles stiffened. "What do you mean?"

Felix perked up and took this one. "Because it's a numbers game. There just aren't enough contract jobs for the clubs to sustain all of the Rangers, or pension funds to pay all of them. There are only so many good-paying, steady spots, in the Rangers Guild and the whole economy. Especially with gear tech and medical tech making everyone live longer, the plan for older, established people to cycle out and allow others to advance doesn't actually work like it was planned."

"Yeah, and Im from a Causeway, no dosh for dat, plus I look like I been kilt once. So I ent gettin no club spot over no one. Scuze me sayin so sir. Ent even got enuff dosh to try really, juss figgaed dat one out lass week. S'lookin like the ol freeknifey way for me."

"Well, young cynical sir, since it's so impossible, I suppose you don't want me to offer you a job."

"Wot, are ye?"

"I could. I am bringing young Loba and my trusted companion Tommy to assist, but I could use three additional hands. With pay for all."

"Huh. Wot den?"

"It's a club contract, but I can bring as many subs with me as I want. Adrenopomes, standard rate per. As many as you can carry."

Now Vic laughed, and thumbed at Jimmy. "Oh, wow. Danks. No danks tho. Sounds fun en all, but I already paid for dis one, en we gonna get nowehere pickin fruit."

"Mhmm, see boy?" he said to the younger Ranger under his wing. "Like I told you before, even when it's offered right to them, some of you youngsters, you just can't take good advice. It's something different about your generation, I swear. Loba, you're saving yourself some time," the man said to his silent protégé, who just nodded after a second. The lack of verbal response was contagious and the convo broke down for a second.

"To each their own," Felix offered.

"Oho, sounds like a toast! And look at that, it's about that time. Five minute call." the older ranger said robustly, rustling in his pouch. These guys were going a bit farther, out to the next stop Felix inferred. They themselves were due to drop in less than two, meaning if what he sensed was right he had little time.

"Indeed!" Felix said, perking, "And what was your name, good sir?"

"I am called Donagan, Jungle Corps, Rank 12, badge 789, lieutenant, Big Game Legion! And in desperate need of a morale boost. Would you like one?" he proffered a hollowed crab shell, the size of his hand, fitted with a stopper and hopefully a wineskin on the inside.

"Well I—"Felix had his own flask, but if he took one of this man's now he'd have more of his own for later. He leaned forward to accept and Vic pushed his hand down.

"Were all fine ova here, danks."

"Fine then. Tis moosewine, a Ranger tradition, but no matter. What are you going for, anyway?"

"Pref not to say." Vic shot a pointed glance at his counterpart sitting next to Donagan.

"Suit yourself. Ha! I can also remember the days when Rangers would actually *talk* to each other about Ranging, instead of all of the cloak and dagger."

"Yeh, well. If I could afford the cloak." Vic said. He leaned back to close the conversation, feigning relaxation, looking tense. Ranger Donagan gave a knowledgeable tut-tut and uncorked the crabshell, pouring the liquid into three little wood snifters. He passed one either way. Felix watched the liquor with longing.

"Alright boys, to steady work!" he said, and upended his drink, shuddering with cheer. Loba did the same. Tommy, the Zuri, froze instead though, looking across the way. It was then Felix noticed their new friend Jimmy was still bent forward, not staring off, fully fixated on the better equipped version of his self across the way.

Donagan noticed the half of this on his side. "Tommy, bup bup, tis bad luck if we don't all do it." Nodding at the little cup in his warrior's hand. Tommy flashed an evil glare back at Jimmy, who was still cooking him optically. He sniffed, and then tilted the drink, and Jimmy said a word.

"*Unlurn.*" It sounded like. And spoken from the heart.

All six of them (and several others in earshot) stopped talking. No one knew the translation, but it was a grave Zuri insult, a prelude to blood and drawn blades putting everyone on notice, considering that the quarters couldn't be closer.

The warrior Tommy choked on his drink. He gulped and let his face descend to rage. He sized up Jimmy for weaponry and checked his own knife on his lap, very deliberately not moving his hand to it, yet. He shifted his around at everyone watching him, and then back to Jimmy.

As far as Felix could see now, Jimmy didn't actually have a weapon on him, which they might have wanted to ask about before they left.

A hail of harsh syllables drilled out of Tommy's mouth in *the* Zuri native tongue that only Jimmy there could understand:

TOMMY: Close your flap and quickly. Young one, I am Tomicohtencatl, on quest from the Mother Red Panther. My lifequest goes sixteen seasons. Tell me who are you are, who says this word to me.

JIMMY: A true son of the forest still. Cauhjimmociuitl of the sacred White Crow. My lifequest only began. My eyes and flap are wide open.

TOMMY: I see. Now, what are you trying to do here by baiting me to murder you and crash this fly-demon-box, young one? Impress the boys you travel with?

JIMMY: I do not think of the safety of this fly-demon-box. I just call you what you are, brother. You drink the City poison and forget the jungle. I see it is working. I am your reminder.

TOMMY: You are lucky my fool here pays me so well, or I would shred the asshole on your face upon the dull side of this sword.

JIMMY: Which side is that? I cannot tell. All I see is equally dull.

TOMMY: You are seriously asking for it, aren't you? Death craves your taste. You must be new, so I am trying to find a reason to not end you.

JIMMY: We all do what we must in this life.

TOMMY: Do not throw scripture at me. You sound like a dickless priest, while I try and speak reason to you. You will come to see how things are. The fools have built a great blasphemy for a homesite and have no idea how to live outside of it, no gods to guide them. My fool is a fine one, he pays me steady to walk him in circles and hunt small, easy things a child could. Your fools? They will not live long, you see, they will lead you to death. You find a fine fat city-pig like mine, he wants your work, you are hungry, you will drink the city poison too if he insists. It is not so bad. We are still Zuri. Still on lifequest. And yours just begins, obviously, so I will let it continue, if you speak no more.

JIMMY: I have said what I need to. Your speech reveals it. You are lost on your lifequest. You would feel my entrails with your hands if it were not true, to prove it. You sit instead, because you are afraid to lose your precious fool's money. Everything you just said is a lie you have told yourself. This is why you are what I say. *Forgetter.*

The word again. Tommy stopped talking, his face sank to grim and he squeezed his fist. Jimmy, barely moving, shifted his center of gravity to aim dead ahead. People started backing up. The two bent towards each other, like a bow tautening. Everyone in the Aero knew enough Zuri to know what was bound by generations of tribal ways to happen next.

Then a whistle blew. A wave of perfume and Regina was back, interposing her hips between the two snarling men.

"Uh uh! No Zuri-on-Zuri, not on my ride!" She clapped her hands three times, hard. "Come on guys, sit back. Both of you. Seatbelts on." She crossed her arms and tapped a foot til they both clicked and complied. Felix leaned back, relieved.

"Good. Now, if you can wait two more minutes, the *effing amateurs* can spill out at the Crevasse, and you three can go rape whatever part of the jungle you're bestowing with your presence today. Any questions?"

"Luv, we neva got our free health potions." Vic said.

"Don't effing speak to me." she said, stalking away to apologizing to the other startled riders. He sneered after her.

Donagan puffed and chortled. "Hoo! You three. Watch it lad, you got a feisty boy there, trying to pick a fight with

Tommy here— Boy! What tribe are you from?"

"White Crow."

"Ah, I'll look out! I may wish to hire a hothead like you for a bout in the Pits!"

Tommy, restrained and bitter about being insulted, saw his opening.

"Ha!" he said with a mean smirk, "If thou can findeth any others."

Donagan gave a brief chuckle, then there was a second of silence. Then the alarms popped off. The light bar beveling the Aero's ceiling began to pulse, a klaxon started klaxing. A minute til first the drop.

As the light went red and the first-timer instructions began flipping on the roloboards, Jimmy hit the buckle button and rammed forward, landing on Tommy's chin fist first. The whole craft wobbled and the crowd went ballistic, equally pushing in and trying to get away from the fight, causing more turbulence.

Vic rose with a pejorative word and tried to insert himself. Tommy pushed up with the wall and heaved Jimmy back off of him, knocking both back into their seats. The older Zuri's dreadlocked head bent at the ceiling when standing, towering over. That dagger came unsheathed.

"Are you all 'touched?" Regina screamed, dashing up to them. "You're going to effing roll us! That door is about to open!"

Jimmy lunged back heedlessly, catching Tommy in the stomach with a punch and grappling his knife hand. Vic was up again, wrapping his arms around Jimmy's waist.

" Ay! Stop, I fookin paid ye, mate!" he said, getting shoved as the two slammed each other around.

"Bruv, help!" he cried to Feix in the same breath.

"What do you want me to do!?" he watched the knife, in

an arm wrestle at waist level. He fretted there for a second behind the twisting melee.

He was still thinking when all the sound of the fight got towed out as the door gasket released and the screaming sky rushed in. It crept open on a hidden wheel, filling the transport cabin with buffeting wind, and leaving nothing between them and a two thousand meter drop.

Vic tried pulling one more time. Felix was still trying to figure out where to best place his efforts, with hands and bodies flying at each other everywhere.

Stop, stop, Vic was yelling, Regina was yelling too, a total chaotic impasse, when someone caught a second wind or got a good angle. Jimmy was flung back. Felix flinched out of the way. He stepped, and got dangerous-close to the gaping door. In terror he wobbled and reached back into the Aero. He wrapped his fingers around something, but he was already too far— foot touched cloud and his body followed, toppling into the air.

VI

He was normally a nervous jumper, so actually this was the quickest Felix had ever cleared a takeoff. He fell out backwards, giving him an excellent view of the ship's underbelly as the wings slid past. As the sun flared out from behind the shrinking craft, he had time to notice what he had grabbed for support was the ticket-taker girl with the angry green eyes.

She flailed and twisted before getting her head pointed down. He was floored with the horrible thought he had pulled her out without her chute, but a few seconds later her hand went to the rip cord at her breast. The air-catching sheet popped out and Felix fell away another two hundred feet before he flipped over and followed suit. The parachute hitting the air felt like the grasp of large talons sliding over and around his shoulders. His fall was arrested and the whistling wind slowed in his ears. He couldn't see her directly above him, but by twisting and craning he saw two other chutes expanding him high to the left.

As soon as he was sure he hadn't just pulled someone to their death, he looked around, trying not to miss a second. Getting up early, Vic's incessant haranguing, the fees of transit and the jungle's perils, this was all worth it for the five minutes between the Aero and the earth. For these few minutes he didn't have to be anyone, or have any answers. This was what the Founders had seen on their first approach to the lake in the valley. A world nude of anyone else's harmful imaginings. He wondered how that moment felt, when they realized they had a second chance. He longed for it fantastically. Like anything he wished he had the ability to reshoot his life's trajectory. Most people in Heaven were lucky to get one shot at a good life though, let alone two. He threw his chance away already. The fortunate birth, the clear path forward. He had given it up and wouldn't get another, and he knew well enough he was not a hustler like Vic who could create his own from nothing. His job at the department store kept him working almost all of his waking hours. There, he was barely holding onto a job, much less thinking of it as a way to advance himself. If he tried to get a Ranger's license like Vic, his overeducated ass would be laughed out the door before they'd hand him the test. Same as just about anywhere he applied. Normal people didn't get much chance to express their distrust of the Wizards face to face often. He could dress scruffy as he wanted and an average shopkeep or manager could still see it on his face still somehow, the shine of privilege they never had, and reflected it back with a scowl. And his father made it clear what would happen if he wanted to come back to the Wizarding life in the Colleges. All of Heaven was a city of refugees in this new land, and Felix doubly so.

So bereft of a plausible, satisfying idea for the future, Felix wasn't quite sure what he was living for anymore. Even the pleasures of Heaven's unlimited bar scene were starting to wilt. He was just trudging through the hours, usually steps behind Vic, feeling less and less like there was any place in the world for him.

He squeezed the taut cords holding his shoulders and looked down at it. Heaven and its lake-straddling Causeways back to the east was a gray smear, getting lost in the monsoon mist.

He fell towards an emerald canopy squeezed by the impassable black cliffs that defined the Valley. The obsidian walls reached higher than any Aero could fly, cradling the jungle between two upturned palms. At some point far down the range, past the Zuri homelands, past the engorged middle swamps where the Ebullio river pirates dwelt in their lawless havens, past even the holy *Copa* tree where the Zuri pilgrimmed, and where the terraced temples of the Royal Alien Blood Empire were rumored to stand, a titanic aquifer poured the down to form the relentless waterway that split and meandered through the valley's bed. It eventually deltaed and bayoued out into the lake Heaven claimed, before seeping into the salt-estuaries to the southeast and joining to the dead, bone-peeling waters at the continent's shore.

The objective beauty of it hit him every time somehow, soothed the dark knot of his mind with a blissful knell. Just for a second. As soon as he let his brain relax, it started prepping for what Regina would say, and whether Vic'd be mad at him, etc., and then he was more than halfway down, and started feeling bad about how he had wasted the best part of the trip overthinking and worrying, with nothing to show for it.

As he shed the last five hundred units of altitude, a bass thud growled his chest cavity. In the mid sky, rapidly getting angled out of view by the tree line, a low hanging patch of cloud imploded into a Storm patch, swollen dark at the middle. The dark gradient in the center strobed bruisy purple and glowed, blinding worms of orange light bled out through creases in the cloud and then burst, sending ball lightning and stria rays marauding cross the surrounding clouds. The crazed shine lit the rainy air like a second sun, dousing the ground beneath with its weird energy.

VII

The drop site was a natural clearing that had been divested of its largest trees, forming a rugged ring. He smacked into ground and went to his knees, chute billowing down behind him.

His first thought was how strong that Storm was. His excitement forked with dread as he reached for his Storm-reader. It was missing. His empty pockets were flush against his leg and he went clammy, thinking of Vic's reaction.

There was a whush down behind him.

"You *prick*!" She was fussing with the carabiners at her shoulders, trying to unclick them with her glamour nails.

"Ugh! What are you doing? Help! First you pull me out of an effing Aero, almost *kill* me, and now you're just standing there? Help! Cummon!"

"It wasn't my fault! I was trying to stop the fight, I got pushed too!" he said as he fled to her and undid the clips, flinching as waved her arms to speak.

"You *grabbed* me! Your dimlit Zuri pal and bustface friend—" two more bumps touched down—" just got me *legit fired*! Do you understand? What are you doing, help me here, get me out of this thing! By the time I'm back they'll have hired someone else, those bastards! This is your fault!"

"I thought you said you didn't care about it?"

"Yeah, that doesn't mean I didn't *need* it, you *privileged* asshole. You don't understand! Now I'm out in the jungle, *completely* unprepared. Are you going to take me back to the boats? Are you?"

"Ayy! Wotsit say!? The reada, dat Storm!" Vic ran up, breathless.

"I...think it got lost," Felix said, getting it out on the third attempt.

"Mate, you wot!?"

"I had it up there! It must have fallen out of my pocket when I fell!"

"Da *fook!* I *knew* I shoulda held it! Ye—" He stopped, and vented his anger into the sky, pulling his hair and stomping around a little bit.

"I'm sorry man! I had it!"

"Um, *hello?* It's cute and all watching you two fight about your toy, but how about taking me the eff to the river, now."

Vic rounded on her. "Not *fookin* likely, luv. Were here to range, til night. Dunno what youre gon do."

"She can follow us—"

"She fookin cant! How can ye not git it, dis my job bruv, I ent a fookin nursemaid! I already have *you* to look out for, I dont needa loudass chick who ent never been out heres follwin us around too! Oh, and *you*—" he got in Jimmy's face.

"Howsit goin, blud? Got anyting a fookin say for yeself?"

Jimmy with his arms crossed, shrugged and gave a noncommittal grimace.

"Toucheth me not during fights. Was fine."

Vic sighed angrily, then gave him a quizzical look, taking a step forward, examining him.

"Fine being a—wait— wheres ya bow?"

Jimmy sniffed. "I use one not."

"Mate, ye ent gotta bow!?"

"Is cheating. For cowards with no hand-fight."

"Ye said ye had gear! Wot, you gotta net?"

"No."

"Sling?"

"No."

"Well, wot den?"

"Just hands. Best way."

"Are you *sure* you done a Shovelbill, bruv?"

"Yes. Good eating."

"Sure, but how the fook ye catch em?"

"Trees. These shovelbirds you call. Loveth the Olli trees. Big time loveth the Olli berries. So findeth first the Olli tree, then climbeth. Then waiteth."

"Uhhh," Regina asked, screwing her face up. "for how long?"

"Until bird is beneath."

"So wot, days? Weeks, in the tree?"

"Yes."

"But Olli trees only bloom in the dry season, right?" said Felix.

Jimmy shrugged again and poked his head up a bit. "Truth. I sayeth so up there, on map, you listeneth not. No birds here."

"Oh." Felix said, his thoughts pivoting. "Well, if that's the case, and we don't want to go back with an empty canister—"

"No, no; shut up bruv." Vic said, shaking his head. "Were not spendin all day takin smoke breaks and pullin styupid slugs off the cliff, forget it."

"I just don't—"

"Bruv, I knew allat, bout the styupid trees. I know its off-season, dats why the price is up. And were not gonna sit around in trees for days, dats obvo, so I was juss tryna—nevahmind, innit. Fook dis." He slammed his jaw shut and strode over to his sprawled out chute, started rolling it.

"What Vic?" Felix said.

"Im goin. I know where. You can come or not, or go to the stupid slug cliffs or straight back home, but I got work to do." He straightened the long straps and click-reeled them back into his pack with a cross look.

Felix teetered over his friend.

"You don't have the reader." He said quietly, hating to remind him. "And it looks like a Storm day. It's not safe."

"Fook it." Vic said, packing up. "*Ye.*" He pointed at Jimmy. "Yer wiff me, where I say, or you can gimme back dat dosh I slid ye."

Jimmy eyed him, before grunting dropping his head and setting to work on the chute.

"Good, least Im gittin *some* backup." Vic said, straightening and shouldering his pack.

"Of course I'm coming with you." Felix said. "I'm here, aren't I?"

"Uh huh." Vic mouthed. He started walking. Felix moped backwards and hastened to roll his chute up as Jimmy walked to follow Vic. Regina was doing the same.

He turned to her. "Are you coming with us?"

"I can't very much make it through the effing *tribal land* alone, can I? Creep. Make them wait for me!"

They did a quick job straightening out their chutes and engaged the auto-retractors. By jogging they caught up with the other two, nearing the mouth of a trail scurrying into the ancient forest they walked toward.

"So, do you assholes have names, or..." Regina said as they met up.

"Jimmy, Felix, Veek." Vic said, spitting the names out as

he flicked his finger around.

"Charmed." she said, eyes doing a full rotation.

VIII

"Hey, so Jimmy, what did that guy say to you?" Felix asked the back of the Jimmy's head. He savored the sound of his words over the hushed timbre of the jungle, no whirr of traffic undershooting his words, a rare relief. He sucked in the moist, sweet air.

"Lies. Protecteth he his mind. Calleth I him out. I am not wrong." he said between stomps.

"No, yeah, of course not— after that I mean, at the end, before you launched on him."

The barbarian took a few steps to respond. "His joke: bad. But he was not wrong either."

"There aren't many White Crow left?"

"Ten men, six women when leaveth I for life-quest. Now?" another shrug.

For fear of being punched, and for knowledge of history, Felix didn't ask what happened. For thousands of years, the Zuri tribes coexisted in a hierarchy modeled after the jungle's own— so sometimes the Red Bears made raids against the Fervent Eagles, or the Swine Rooters would bicker over territory with the Clan of the Yamtree, but no one really feared going extinct. Two hundred years ago, the City unbalanced things. It wasn't a matter of taken territory, none of the tribes had cared about the barren stone in the middle of the lake before then, and the Demarcation Treaty had made bloody sure they stayed there— only the lawbreaking Homesteaders had dared to cross the verboten lake line. Those ones were reviled equally by the tribes and almost all the Cityfolk as well. No, without conquering an acre, the economic stimulus of Heaven next door had rearranged tribal life, made every homesite a competitor against the rest. The life-quest thing was part of it. At adolescence, according to Zuri custom the vigorous young men of a tribe were ceremonially exiled, to return to tribal life only after they had accomplished or at least satisfied their ambitions— literally making a new name for themselves to wear through their remaining years. There were other factors having to do with trade and politics, but the hard truth was that a huge percentage of young men came to live, work, and die in the City without ever finishing their life-quest. As the number of young men returning to tribal life dropped, the tribes adapted to soak up those who did, with many laxing longheld ideas on alcohol, sex, and other pleasurable bits of life that had always existed but never been a problem until they became available commercially. Others tightened up, appealing to true believers. And despite all this, many tribes shriveled, became examples. Now culture clash was the norm in the lower valley and extinction was its byword.

"That sucks man, I'm sorry."

"Is what tis. But is not funny."

"Yeah, not like you guys dropping your little Stormreader after worrying about it getting stolen!" Regina said, trying to get a reaction, but Felix just dropped his head in defeat.

"See, that's how I know you're definitely a richkid Wizard, I would've been practically *stabbin* myself if I lost something that cost that much."

"I learned the 'be quietly guilty' coping mechanism instead, I guess."

"Ew. I mean, how much was that stupid thing, anyway?"

"A bleedin thou and some. Nuff for a months rent." Vic gritted out.

"A thou! Eff me*hehehehehehe!*" Regina burst out, the world dissolving into sustained giggling. "Haaa!"

"Sorry, sorry— but that's just ridiculous. I never even looked at them that close, wow. I mean, what did that little thing do that was worth an effing *thou?*"

"It had dials that tell you how strong, how close, and how likely the next Storm will be. And it alerts you when a Storm is about to break, too." Felix said, accepting the punishment.

"Alerts you? Like, it beeps?"

"Yeah."

"Oh, see, nah! That sounds stupid. Little storms happen all the time, it'd probably go off right when you're about to like, make a stealth kill out here, right?"

"That's why you can set the sensitivity high, like I did," Felix said, a little edge on his voice now. "You make it only ring for really big or really close Storms, that's blatant."

"Alright, fine, just tryna make you feel better. Sounds like, not that important."

"Shows whatcha know, luv. Its to put you in the sweet spot, innit. Or it was."

"Sweet spot?"

Felix answered. "The ring around any given Storm, where you're not going to get hit, but you're close enough to run in get the first chance to hunt anything that did."

She shook her head, and let him step ahead of her again.

"And that's what you Rangers do out here? Great. Effing idiots."

"It's better than just walking straight into one." Felix said.

Vic gave a wry caw of a laugh.

IX

The dropsite and the well-worn path they walked were the territory of the Rock Sloth Zuri, one of Heaven's most docile and familiar trade partners. They made good time to the Zortell Crevasse. Thirty minutes on it was obvious they were close as trees shrank and a plate of stone could be felt beneath the springy soil. They came into a clear rise of weathered rock cantilevered out over a ravine. On the other side of the drop, a gray cliff towered tall next to the little pad of stone they stood on.

The Zortell Crevasse was a known location for junior rangers and part-time junglers. It was safe. The huge rock above it jutted out and from the view you were right over the river, could jump straight in if your deathwish was strong enough. In case it wasn't, the overhang also served as a natural shelter big enough to hide out from a Storm if you got caught in one. At the bottom, mouths of black caverns yawned down into the earth. Felix and Vic had gulped over the Ranger Reports and the treasures extracted from within. Faceted fistules of milky blue stone. Hides of terran lurkers that curled and smoked when exposed to daylight. High bounty stuff—they could only dream of the equipment they'd need.

That's not why most people came here. The Crevasse's sun-fraught wall was a gathering place for regislugs, tubular annelids that came to the surface to absorb the day's heat before crawling back into the recesses they etched out of the rock with weak acids in their body. They grew up to a foot long, camouflaged into the rock, and were used by factories to make ink for the Wizards, who might as well have been drinking it for the level of constant demand. You could basically exchange them directly for cash at any time of the year. It was pretty mindless work, which is why it made a safe bet for amateurs like they.

The Zortell slugs— named for their home's discoverer — were found to possess natural pigments and compounds which could be refined to a room temp opal liquid that could carry a thaumatic charge, to the delight of the Wizards and unknowing dismay of the slugs. The rock face dripped with rappelers, scathing their way down the wall, to pull the beasts out of their holes, wearing special gloves, shoving them into Cuum-cans to await extraction.

The bootprints in the mud bifurcated here. To the right, the trail would skirt the deep part of the Crevasse and lead to the top of the slug rocks. Left, down into a lowland, the open jungle.

"Lookaddem. Sluggin the day away forra few skint bills. *Slaves.* Paffetic." Vic said, pausing to survey, without acknowledging they had been dangling from that wall the week before. He pulled his map out for a quick consult.

"Cummon, this way," he said after a beat, looking up to double check the trail marker, picking a trailhead leading further west.

Jimmy made a grunt, staring at the horizon over the trees.

"Wot, wot now?"

Jimmy frowned and searched the sky for a second. He popped his knuckles and listened to how they crunched, then shook his head in disapproval. "Storm-day. Air feeleth full."

"Yeh, dere was a hit like, a half hour ago, so wot."

"No. In air. Still full. Heavy."

"Ye full of it mate, no one can feel a Storm comin, dats why dey suck, innit."

The young warrior looked at them like they were dumb. "Zuri can. True Zuri."

"Never hearda dat— when den? Where at?" Vic said.

"Knoweth not. Feeleth only."

"Well, I *knoweth* I cant afford to pay ye and go back with nuffin, so— if ye feared, gimme dat money back now and head forra boat wiff dis one here, straight up." He gestured at Regina.

"Ooh, yes! Please choose that! Who here doesn't want to get turned into a flyer today?" Regina said, raising her pointy hand.

Jimmy turned to Vic, grim.

"Offereth I guidance. As *guide* you hireth. You listen not? Fine. But feareth? No. Never feareth."

Felix didn't say what he was thinking, that there was still plenty of space on the cliff, if they were worried about going back empty-handed, and Vic was thinking about their finances. Sticking with a sure thing for another week or two might be a safer plan. He stood there and waited for the others to make a decision.

"Good to fookin hear. Right den, wot are we standin round for?" Vic said, withdrawing his machete from a sheath in his backpack, and turning toward the brushy, vine-choked path.

X

They quieted up as they battled down the trail, which soon dwindled into a narrow brown line mushed through the underbrush as they curved away from the overlook and down the soaked descent. The air stunk with the humid head trapped beneath the canopy. Felix wished like anything he had that Storm-reader. Until very recently, even expert storm trackers used little more than guess-work. The invention of the handheld Storm-reader was widely talked about. Felix followed Storm news with a morbid level of curiosity. He had to have one, starved himself for weeks to save enough and not miss a rent check.

The purpose of the device was to help users avoid or find the spots where creatures touched by a Storm's rays were most likely to be. From all the radiant, ram-parting, thousand-hued beauty of the valley, the Storms stood above all. They were a new phenomena the Founders had discovered after arriving in the Valley, and they had remained unexplained since. Random swell-ups of an un-known, undeniable energy tore great glowing rifts across the vault of the clouds, to seal and silence minutes later. They weren't really storms at all— whatever they were though, they started in the low sky and drew the rain and lightning into a swirling radius, so storms they were called. They were sublime enough just to witness—towers of bearded clouds rushing to assemble, a jubilee of colored lights exploding in the stria beneath, cyclones braiding the edges, the whole massive event limned with coppery-orange godhead tracing out into the surrounding sky.

It was what the Storms did for which they were feared and valued. The rays that fell instilled themselves in whatever they touched, and changed it. Minerals metamorphosed, melted, crumbled to salt in seconds. Most living creatures caught in it were liquefied, but some were altered less extremely. Their coats and feathers sprang out in garish new colors, heads spouted second rows of teeth, necks sprouted second heads. Storm-touched beasts fetched the most rival of prices with top-cat buyers—high line chefs, wizard-academics performing unique experiments, couturistas seeking furs of the first quality. Plants were for some reason unaffected, except when struck by actual lightning, in which case they typically caught on fire.

What happened to people caught in these thaumatic occurrences wasn't as spectacular. No flamboyant physical shifts. You just went crazy. There was a property to that energy that scrambled the conscious brain so it could never be set right again. You were just Storm-touched then. 'Touched. A flyer, if you were less sensitive, for the unceasing urge they got to flap their arms off the nearest rooftop.

There was little left of you after. The 'touched wandered into the jungle, never to return on a riverboat, or they disappeared more obliquely. Unless the case was reported for treatment to the Wizards in time. *Like someone had done for that woman that morning. Like his sister, plus all the others in the labs, beneath the subfloors of the Edifice College—*

Nope, he told himself, shutting those thoughts down before it took control of him.

Don't think about it.

They made it thirty minutes down the jungle slit before Regina startered making complain-y noises about the heat and the mud. Vic shushed her for this, which begat an exchange of rapidfire insults/getting-to-know-you questions, as the two sussed out each other's connections and affiliations within the city, all for which they fell on rival sides, opinions opposing. They built on their base loathing of each other's neighborhoods with more specialty disagreements about the political du jour— Regina was pro-South Bank, Vic anti-. He called her an efficient cock-user for her pro-birth control stance. She implied that Rangers had an intelligence maximum for their entrance requirements. By the time The Expansion Question came up, they assumed (correctly) that this was a non-starter as well.

"S'gonna happen, any mans who dont tink so is *'touched,* or an idyot child, innit."

"Kay, so you're like, a full-on warmonger. *Wow.*"

"Try practical luv. I have *eyes.* The city is *full,* but the youfs keep comin. No one realize it growin up— but dey aint enuff jobs, no place to put anyone else. If ye tink Heaven can stay the same size foreva, ye dreamin."

"And you're *an effin dimlit* if you think that expanding the borders will do anything but start a war. Like, it's not empty space."

"Yeh but we would prolly win tho."

"Oh yeah, sure. Against all the Zuri, who are our *allies* by the way— *plus* the Ebullio, *plus* the Shreklie, *plus* the RABE —"

"The RABE dont even fookin exist, the Wizards made dem mans up, s'a threat to scare dimlits, like you, ovvo— And the rest, I mean, have ye seen wot the new strapshots can do on 'chop' mode? No question, innit? No offense, Jimbo. Heaven's gettin bigga."

Jimmy snorted. "Tryeth. Never bigger than jungle."

" Well see! Nah. One day soon, jussayin. Look, I dont wannit to go down either, but Im a realist, and theres no way were gonna void it."

Regina persisted. "You know we're not actually running out of *space*, right? It's resources. Everyone in the city, especially the *rich*,"— she jagged a look at Felix— "consumes too much. Food, water, solar. We don't have to start a war, we just need to get everyone to stop using more than their share. Then the city will never have to expand, and mongers like you can die disappointed."

"*Ehhhhhhhhhhnh.*" Vic made a sound like a quiz show buzzer. "If ye tink *erryone* in Heaven will evah agree on anyting enuff to do dat, yer more naïve den I thought. S'happenin, I swear it."

"Expansion would be barbaric. Maybe I just have hope for a less bloody solution."

"You want a lot of people to die, but dont want to see any blud, luv?"

"Um, no. Less death I said, less death."

"So how do ye expect to fix overpop wiffout gettin ridda some people??"

"Um, like I said, better planning for the future. That means birth control. That means rations, limits on consumption, especially in the Colleges. Better agricultural efficiency on the lake farms, less waste. A max one kid per fam for a few generations might be a good idea too."

This caught Felix's attention. "You think the Wizards should be in charge of the birth rate? What would you do with all of the second and third kids that got born on accident?" he said, for the sake of debating.

"Someting not bluddy, deffo."

"So *you* think we should steal the Zuri's lands too." Regina said to Felix.

Felix shrugged. "Oh, no, that definitely won't work either."

"So what's your solution?"

"I don't have one— I'm just getting through life. Trying to enjoy it."

She scoffed. "Ugh, you're even worse than him then, barely. A privileged-ass Wizard kid with no concept of the struggle and an ignorant wannabe Ranger warmonger from effing Merit, great."

"Don't forget the angsty, hardline Zuri kid and the spazmouth broad from Freedom with the same opinion as every other social justice warrior on the island."

"Okay, go eff yourself, if I share opinions with anyone, it's because we're *right.* I can dress however I want, speak out about whatever issue I feel like, be as poly as I want with whoever I choose, and *act* however I want, and you can't shame me for it. This is a society built on *freedom*, but everyone forgets that as soon as a woman says something contradictory. When did social justice become a bad thing anyway? I mean, I'm not allowed to join the Rangers because I'm a girl, right off the bat— and how many female Wizards are actually in positions of power in the Pyramids? Like, four. There is no good opportunity for women in this society if you don't want to be a waitress til you break a hip, or be someone's wife to plop out babies, which is obviously a problem you acknowledge too, so, *excuse me* for *talking loudly* about how jacked up it all is to be a girl out here. No one listens at a normal volume."

"Did you just say yer poly? *Hmm.*" Vic responded immediately.

"Uhhhh, did you say that we were actually *going somewhere?* If it's much farther, you picked the wrong drop site, or more likely have no idea where we are. Effing typical." her coif was melting off one side of her humid head. Her iPhly jacket was insulated for the high winds, and hung heavy and damp on her. Floes of undereye makeup smeared on her cheeks.

"Still a while, patience, patience. Feelin hot, luv? S'good look for ye."

"Dude, you are effing *beyond* help. Like, I'm trying to decide which of the things I'm carrying to stab you with right now."

Vic dismissed this with a hard laugh and they fell back into quietness, now just ignoring Regina's ughing. They slunk through the jungle for close to an hour like this, ranging the boundless. sticky landscape, an infinite scroll of glossy leaves and swollen flowers, bell clusters, nectaries, dragon-tongues, pistils by the trillions, licking the steam.

The muggy trudge was hypnotic. Felix's mind played games, imagined nice conversations that couldn't actually happen. He pretended one of his companions asked what they'd all wish to be if the Storms affected people like it did animals. Transformed their bodies, instead of twisting their minds. Vic, he was sure, would want to be something powerful and smart, something no one could eff with— a dragon gator, or a pit chimaera. The others he didn't know so well, so he fast-forwarded the conversation to how he might answer.

The first thought was pretty depressing— in all of his fantasies, he was just nothing— something that took up no space or had any volume, nothing at all. He thought about this a lot. Not like, he wanted to kill himself, that would essentially prove everyone right about him, but he would, he had decided, take the choice to phase out of existence as if he'd never been, if it were given. He had gotten a bird's eye view of all of the paths through life, and in the last year a worm's perspective too. Nothing he could be or do seemed better or worse than any other options, all tasted like dust to future him. Most people wanted to be happy, but he knew just what happiness was, a bodily response to validation, a moment's distraction from the City, trapped in its own walls. So he had stopped seeking or expecting it from his life at all. He had learned enough to make himself an alien in his own home, an unskilled bag of gruesome, depressing facts about the WSWN, that had dropped out before he was anywhere near the levers of Wizard power to enact any sort of change. Not that the City wanted to change. Or that he would have had any clue about the WSWN if he hadn't dropped out, stayed in the insulated world of the Colleges. So he was doomed and useless no matter what he did. *You brought all of this pain on you.* He made sure to remind himself all the time.

As noon came, they were still walking, Vic filled the air more and more frequently with justifications and reassurances that their destination was near. It was a relief to all of them when these murmurings peaked in excitement. Vic rushed forward.

"Lookaddit! Olli saplin! *Ayy!*"

Sure enough, the path ahead shot up between two steep slopes, forming a gully awash in shiny new growth green, studded with a galaxy of white flowers. It jumped out from the baroque foliage of the old growth behind and around, immediately a strange sight, seeing hundreds of the same tree planted next to each other. In stark contrast to the swarming brushy tangle they came through, this bit looked more like a place in the City. Mulched trunks flattened the underbrush, and trapped heat in the soil. The place had a stink of a killing ground, aerobic body fluids and animal musk percolating in their flared nostrils.

"Were here!" Vic cried out.

"Fucketh." Their guide stopped, murmuring Native words under his breath and making a hand symbol over his chest.

"What is this, Vic?" Felix said, anxious and awestruck.

"A aeekrit Ranger ting bruv.we found it! Deys got mans coming out here, gassin the soil up with Wizard farm chems I heard, now the Ollis bloom a few weeks heada the dry season."

"What is that smell?"

"Predator pellant— keeps anyting big away, and the birds cant smell anyting, no noses bruv."

Felix's eyes zipped to the even tree plantings, the hauled in mulch, the man-made shack, out alone in the jungle.

"Vic, is this place sanctioned?"

"Sure, by Rangers, deffo."

"Doubt it. I know all of the sanctioned out-of-City sites from my job, my *former* job, and I've never heard about this one. If this was a real site, there would be a drop site near." Regina said, all a bit muffled as she tried to fit her nose into her jacket.

"Well... its special. Some arrangement with the tribe here. I dunno, I juss clocked it listenin in da Guild Hall bruv."

"Vic— that means this is homesteading man, poaching. If there is any sort of deal, it's some backdoor thing between whoever is bringing fertilizer out here and the tribe. This is an unsanctioned, illegal settlement site. This is breaking the Treaty. We shouldn't be here."

"The Treaty bruv? Cummon. Buv, its almost year 244.

Mans dont care out here! Wizards dont care where the stuff come from. And if they did, wot deygonnado— send the Rangers to arrest themselves? Be real bruv. This the type ting smart people do to get ahead. Plus, look, no ones here! We got dibs!"

He strode into the grove. The Olli trunks, smooth and stretch-marked from their synthetic feed, jousted thirty feet into the sky, terminating in a frond of draping branches that swept down to head height. Juvenile berry pendulums weighted and varied their drift in the sticky wind.

"I been readin. This is early, even for early season— but its been warmer this year, innit? So figure were a little heada the almanacs. Cummon Jimmy, lets get set up."

Jimmy didn't budge from the grove's rim.

"We cannot."

"Oh yeh yeh—I know, I knows, dis kinda ting gonna destroy the jungle, but ye know wot? Its gonna *un*destroy us blud, so Im okay wiff it. Now *shift,* cummon, lets go."

"They will not like that." He said.

"Blud, Im serious, if ye say the Great Crow and his mates —"

"*No* Your folk."

"Wot? Who?"

He jabbed his finger around. "In trees. Sitteth there. There, there. Thereth. There. There."

His digit pointed down the row, wherever it went, the edges of treeblinds, little wooden platforms and hammocks traced themselves out of the background every ten meters or so.

"Where? Ooooh, shite. Fook. shhhh, shh! Dont move!" Vic wavered in the clearing, suddenly embarrassed. He listened, figuring what next, when a whistling crossbow bolt plugged itself into the ground a few feet away. A paper fragment was poked around its shaft. Vic ripped it off and read.

FVCK OFF, ALL TREES TAKEN. BEEN HERE 2 DAYS

."As I had sayethed." Jimmy said to Regina, face unchanging.

"Wot, alla dem? A lotta trees out here— *cummon!*" Vic shouted at the trees, spinning. Another shaft fell from a different direction:

YES. BYE

Vic read the new note and his eyes tightened. He balled his fists and squeezed out a strangle noise like something had burst inside.

Felix dove out and yanked Vic's arm, as a swarm of pointed statements zipped into the ground where he just stood. They kept moving before the shooters could reload, hightailing it back twenty meters, out of range. Felix slowed up, out of breath. Vic followed through with his momentum, and punched an Olli sapling, before tearing off its branches and ripping its roots from the ground. He yelled a little bit more til he ran out of steam and crouched over his knees.

"Wow, so you're like, not even good at this."

"Fook *off!!*"

Felix chuckled.

"Ah come on buddy, its okay. We can fill up on slugs today and try a different spot next weekend for something big. That spot is sketch anyway."

Vic laughed too, but with no shred of humor. He quieted and righted himself. He forced Felix to make eye contact.

"Sometimes bruv, I wonder wot world ye live in."

"Uh, the real, real messed up one, same as you."

"Yeh? S'like ye ent clock how broke we are. Ye gotta

mental fookin block. Dese fookin slugs ent cuttin it bruv, not wiff *yor* lifestyle. Afta ye maff the extra costs we come up shorta and shorta each month— not like it stops ye from drinkin yer cut plus half of erry one ye paychecks, but I dont even try en talk bout dat anymore, innit."

"Whoa, well," Felix said, off-guard, backbone stiffening, taking unawares for a serious convo—. "It's my money and I pay my half of the rent so—"

"Dont matta dat we got the lights bout to turn off, a huge fookin grocery tab, my Ranger dues coming up— fook it. I could use some help here bruv. S'do-or-die ting. If ye and me dont make some money dis trip, tings is gettin cut off. I cant even afford this do-nuffin *Gooli* the other half— I werent gonna fookin hire ye except I felt bad, blud— Like, Im sayin by next week we dont eat, we lose the apartment, or I lose my job, which means all three. Were fooked mate. Were priced out. Were headed for the barges. Were CWs. Im done."

"Hey buddy, come on, we'll figure it out. Let's think."

"Blud, I *have* thought— dats the worst part. We had dis fookin convo last night. I told ye how serious today was, an ye got smash-oed in front of me en dont even rememba nuffin. I cant count on ye bruv. And now look."

"How is any of this my fault? I was just trying to help you on *my* day off."

"Fook bruv! Im not saying it is! Juss dont act like ye ent out here *contributin* to the fookin WSWN ye bitch about en dont chat me off wiff dat 'tings is going to be okay' muleshite. S'really not."

Felix shuffled and looked down. "Sorry man." He had never seen his Vic lose it so hard.

His friend, never one to stop moving long, rolled his neck and picked up his pack.

"Woteva. Cummon. Lets go. We can hunt *something*. We still got time. And if ye have any good ideas, spit em now."

He walked past the torn up sapling, back the way they came.

XI

Felix got that freefall feeling again, less pleasant this time. *So this is when the dream ends*, he thought. This is the brick wall to end his year drunkenly worshipping his own feelings. His brain scuttled around, probing for a rationale, some way to reshuffle the finances or facts of the situation. There was nothing to mortgage further. Not even the Storm-reader to pawn. No way to keep ignoring his own life, and now, the drag he had had on Vic's, which he was just now fully realizing, adding another layer of worry to the stack in his head. He felt like garbage. Even more so, because above it all, he was harboring the thought that he could, if he wanted, walk back to his father's office in the Edifice and ask for his old room back, if he were willing. He'd never say such a thing out loud, but he knew it was true.

"Big crap pile." Jimmy said, interrupting Felix's internal monologue when they were a few minutes up the little path.

"Thanks Jimmy, I know."

"No. Here." His dread bopped against his back muscles as he crouched, furting around in the underbrush. His hand popped above the leaves and called them over.

They were staring at a spongy coil of feces. Jimmy broke after a twig and stirred the pile, releasing a puff of steam. He swiveled his head, eyes active.

"Fresh."

"What made it?"

"Octorilla. Single. Male. One track." He had found a riff in the leaves and studied its contour into the forest, cross-ways to the path.

"Whoa! Cant be far." Vic said, swiveling.

"Hey hey hey," Regina said. "Aren't those things like, a thousand kilos? Not effing likely, for you three."

"Not three. Me. Goeth you three to the River."

"Wot? Im still rentin ye!"

Jimmy pointed at the sun, past its apex.

"Payeth you for half day of killing. Sayeth you you have not the other half."

"Yeh, but if we get a fookin octorilla—"

"*No!*" Jimmy barked, raising his voice. "You are loud. A risk! Goeth I alone." He rocketed his neck around to glare at Vic.

"Parteth we now." He confirmed with a nod, before lop-ing off, using long strides to show they'd been holding him back the whole time.

They watched him go. Vic raged.

"*I hope it fooking rapes ye!*" he yelled after. Incensed, he turned to Felix and Regina.

"Fook him!" he said. As he opened his mouth to rant more, there was a flash between the limbs and leaves be-hind his head. For a moment, the sky was a fiery, opaque lavender, before fading back to overcast slate. Regina and Vic both saw it.

Vic did two 180s.

"Wait, was dat a Storm??" Vic scanned both sides of his hands, making sure he was still there.

A gust of wind hit them in the face. "I don't *think* so..." Regina said, but she crouched.

"It was a pop!" Felix said. This happened sometimes,

rare crackles of the Storm that disappeared as fast as they came, you could miss them if you blinked.

XII

"No way, no way—" Vic twitched his nose. "Smoke! S'close! Mebbe it hit a ting!"

He went crashing through the brush, widening Jimmy's trail. Felix launched after, thoughts still catching up, anxiety rising. Each Storm was a beacon for jungle looters, scumbling for Stormtouched animals to turn into rare goods, anyone could be inbound. But by dumb luck it seemed they had ended up in the sweet spot by accident; it was just they and the forest.

The bellowing roar burst from ahead, chilling Felix's stride. He fumbled for the bow on his back with sweaty hands and tried to keep his eyes on the trees. Fumes made the air thick and hazy. Shapes leapt and danced through the particles. Small packets of flame hung on singed branches and smaller animals crashed around, snakes, monkeys, and marmots streaming away from the site, staggering and chittering pained noises. He caught glimpses of iridescent jewelbox colors mixed in their coats as they fled through the burning treetops.

Bigger shapes moved through the dusky glade. A low hump became Vic, Jimmy was five meters in front, stalking with purpose towards a rocky formation jutting up dead ahead. Felix's gaze drew up to look at the base of the strange rock, and saw something curled down there, shifting, moving.

The shape resolved itself into a head, shoulders, and

multitude of shaggy limbs, its back to them. Two fists whiteknuckled the edges of the boulder, its other four arms heaved and slapped its heaving body, clutching its face. It grunted and made little shrieks.

When the wind shifted, the yellowed smoke peeled off to show its fur had all gone a strange calico—contrasting vermilion, cream, and turquoise.

It lurched about with panic throes, clawing at its face with its two forelimbs. It hadn't seen them yet. Felix got low, and looked around for Regina. He tried to speed up to get to Vic. He tried to nock an arrow to his bow. He tried to keep an eye on the beast at the same time, trying to figure out what was wrong with it, the best way to approach it without being killed, then took a brief tangent to doubt his own decision-making process and completely scrap all of his half-formed tactics.

By the time he reached Vic, Vic had caught up with Jimmy, and Regina had triangulated to the spot too.

"Okay, here's the plan—"

"It hasn't seen us," Felix said.

"I know! So we gotta—"

"I shall challenge. Rillas do not back down." Jimmy said, slipping a rigid object over each hand. When his fingers moved away his knuckles were crenellated with a sharpened ridge of obsidian. He leaned to go.

"Stand back."

"Wot, shh! No, wait. Fookin lissen— You git ready. Ill shoot it in the backada head, try and one-shot it. Felix, you shoot right afta me, just hit it somewhere. Jimmy, ye ent got no bow, I dunno know wot yer gonna to do, just—"

"Killeth with hands."

"It has six *fookin* arms, grow up! We gotta distract it first, try and get behind it or someting. Im goin for the headshot, if that dont work, well juss keep *unloadin* at it, good?" he said to Felix.

"What about me?" Regina hissed.

"Are ye even *fookin armed?*"

"In fact—"

"I dont care, just get the fook away, lemme git dis shot!"

He moved his body into position, and took a deep breath.

"Kay, on three—"

"JUNGLE BROTHER!" Jimmy said, at the top of his lungs, standing up. He made some exaggerated movements towards the ape.

"Jimmy *wotthefookmate*—"

The beast screamed in query. It righted itself, and took its hands away from its face. It twisted the side of its head toward the sound of an enemy. Its whole head was a bloody mess. The six-armed hulk tasted the air with its tongue, stilling, perched on the or of a fight or flight instinct.

"It's blind," Felix told everyone, but his words were just part of the next moment's chaos, when Vic's bow loosed, and the arrow's stalk jerked into the octorilla's shoulder.

"Shite!" Vic yelped at the same time the creature howled. It ripped the arrow out and rocked around, slamming the ground and bouncing aggressively toward them. Jimmy strode forward.

"You idiots!" Regina said, backpedaling.

"Bruv, shoot!"

"I'm trying!" Felix said, hands shaking. He tried to push some wisdom up and the fear down, see the arrow traveling where he wanted. He released and watched the shaft swim past the beast's shoulder.

Vic grunted and let another zip, shooting over Jimmy's ear to stick the beast in its ribs, eliciting another enraged scream but barely slowing the beast.

"Keep goin!" Vic yelled at Felix, but now Jimmy was closing in and blocking a clean shot, turning sideways, getting low, meeting the beast in the scorched clearing. He had the advantage of the octorilla's attention being split, and blinded. But the beast still had a half meter, three hundred pounds, and four arms on the ambitious barbarian. Any one of those muscled limbs had enough power to yank the head off his shoulders.

Felix was beginning to see that Jimmy had a pattern, and really wanted it to continue. He stepped to the left to get a better angle, put an arrow in the air and managed to stick it in the beast's side, but not hard enough to sink the bodkin. The beast barely noticed, and Felix spun his brain for something else to try.

Jimmy roared and rushed the beast. He got close and put a two-fist combo into its spittle-filled maw. Its head rocked each way and the jawbone drooped, but already its forearm were batting him down while the fingers squeezed and tried to find a death grip.

Their friend's next punch didn't have the same panache as he lost momentum. His feet left earth as the octorilla got two hands on him, wrapping around his neck, back, and knees, constricting him sixfold. His body started quaking.

There was lots of wailing at that point, and Felix turned his head to avoid the fuss of the next part. The beast's screeches peaked and sounds crackled out of the back of its throat.

He opened his eyes to see Regina on the beast's left shoulder, shoving a foaming can into its hanging onto a knife plunged into its back and trying to spray a macecan into its eyes. It dropped Jimmy and reached around for her, but its knees wobbled from the assault. An arrow grew from its throat, Vic finally finding his mark.

The long-haired hulk lost its footing. Regina kept stabbing at its spine. Vic rushed in with a long blade, warning her back, and inserted it into the beast's throat. He was rewarded with a volcanic wave of artery blood. That still didn't kill it. Vic got knocked down as the body jerked but he bounced off the hard earth and back up to hack the blade down two handed, whipping it against the beast's neck until the bending metal was sticky and the beast raged no more.

XIII

"WEOOOOOOOHOOOOOOOOOOO!" Vic hollered, flipping the machete out of his hand. Birds scattered upward.

"Bruv! Loo at the coat on dis ting! Annits huge! Were *cakin*. Can ye believe it!?"

"No, not really!" Felix said.

"Ye dont even have to! D'ye know how *set* dis makes us? We can get a new Storm-reader *tomorrow*—all that important life shite too! Nevamind wot I was sayin before, we're all good, cummon, lets tag it."

"Tight!" Felix said.

They slapped hands, sending blood gobs off of Vic. He started strutting like a rooster around the body.

Regina threw down the shriveled mace can, and bent to wipe her arms and hands off in the dirty and remaining plant life. She went to Jimmy, propping himself up.

"Are you okay? Need help?"

"No worry, am fine." Jimmy coughed out, his neck a patchwork of black and purple. He staggered to his hands and knees and vomited into the earth.

"Suit yourself," she said.

"Hes better den okay, hes gettin paid!" Vic said, still parading. "Bruv, look at those extra eyes, the Storm messed its whole face up. A fookin specimen othawise. *Dat hide.*" He stroked a patch of relatively bloodless arm hair.

Regina's eyes rolled. "Gloat more." she regarded the

93

half-ton-at-least carcass. "You idiots do have your own Cuum-can, right?"

Vic's teeth glowed. "S'matta fact—" he whipped a short shiny tube from his pack with great satisfied.

"Oh, why yes, dis *is* the deluxe model from Pagerock, good eye luv! Yes, the kind wiff a extra five cubic meetas of space. Whyd pay for the extra meetas? S'cause I just knew Id be need enuff space to haul back a *full-grown,* Storm-touched octorilla? Nah! Treek question. I *dint* pay for it, s'free, *from the Rangers Guild,* because the Rangers Guild is the a class establishment. haHa!."

"No argument there." she said, pulling out her own, slightly more dinged canister. "But let me get mine first. I bet you're going to whine about the head, so cut off the feet for me and all of the claws and toenails and we'll call it even. Don't front like I don't know what this is worth."

"Wait, why do you have a Cuum-can?" Felix said. "You're not a hunter."

She shrugged. "I collect tech, like I told you."

"Waitwaitwait luv." Vic said. "This is my trip here, who said ye git a cut?"

"*You're* about to get a cut." She said, wiggling her little switchblade, still soupy with gorilla fluids.

"Cheell! Look, wot Im sayin, s'worth more all togetha, I can break ye off some bills *afta* I sell it whole to the Rangers, so—"

"No, now. I don't have any income after this, I'm not leaving it up to you."

"Then ye completely dumb! All we gotta do is git it back to the City. Ye wanna start choppin it into bluddy hunks and pullin its toenails out out here? No!"

"I'd *never* take money from the Rangers Guild."

"Well, *I* can' bring back seven-eigffs of an octorilla carcass! Ill look like an idyot!"

"Hey! Don'tcha wurry much 'bout that naow." a voice said. There was a clic and a swoosh, Then three men with three crossbows were in their midst.

"Mang, these new cloakin' devices actually work! Wizards, pah! Can't keep the city lights to stay on, but dang they make one helluva gadget." said the one with his shooter leveled at Vic's left eye,

"Drop it," another said to Regina re: the switchblade in her hand. He shook her from behind until she complied.

The last one remained silent, and pushed Jimmy to prone on the ground, resting the bolt tip on his brainstem.

They wore jackets patched with scraps of odd fabric, and hats made of skins with the feet and tails still attached. The red bandanas around their necks, they didn't even bother to pull over their faces— half tangled beard, the other half rotting teeth and florid skin. They had tattoos where Zuri wore them but the faces of Heavenites. These announced them as Homesteaders, cityfolk who broke the law and settled illegally beyond the wall at the lake's edge. Despised by city and scourged by the tribes, they survived in feral colonies, hunting and robbing indiscriminately. Felix was a little disheartened to see none of the roughnecks pointing a crossbow at him. He felt minimized, but not for long.

"*Pah.* Awright kid." Vic's new friend spat at Felix to indicate him. "Listen up. Don't do nothing fast or stupid." Felix pondered this, as the bandit explained.

"You just do what I say an' your crew don't get lit up. If youse a selfish type who don't care bout that, please do note, these are some *repeating* crossbows, so we got some for you too if need be. Good?"

He nodded, looking at Vic, his big eye bulging to look at

the would-be murder weapon.

"Good, boy. Now listen close. You don't hafta say nothing. You just gonna take one of those Cuum-cans your friends got, shove that there octoriller in there, and hand it to me all nice like. We won't hurtchas none, just don't say a word and do like that and we'll all be on our way. Alright git naow." Vic made a noise like there might be better options and got kicked to his knees by the talkative member of the Homesteader raiding party.

Felix looked around at the six expectant faces waiting for his next move. He hesitated, hoping some creative answer was about to spring into his mind, but nothing arrived. He bowed his head and stepped slowly to Regina.

He kneeled and picked up the magic storage container, and twisted it open. He looked at the still-warm behemoth one last time, before tapping a button and watching the biggest catch he'd ever been a part of disappear into the tube with a final pop. Vic groaned. Felix turned around and handed the canister to the bandit.

"Ha! Thank you kindly young sir. You rookies did a real fine job on that one. Now, and we hate to be so needy, but there is the matter of any potions, weapons, boots, tech, loot, whatnot you happen to have—"

"You said that all! Please, we're super broke, we really don't have anything—"

The lead bandit leaned out and grabbed his arm, laughing.

"That's what you think *now*, city boy. Trust me it gits worse. Now strip, all youse, throw it in a pile."

He didn't offer any alternatives besides close range archery. Felix dropped his bow, and pulled his half-empty flask out, hands shaking, deciding if he should chug the last few mouthfuls, wishing now, more than anything, that he had found time for one last drink. He foisted it down and clapped out the crap his pockets for anything else, but really had nothing else left.

As they were shaking down the others, there came a beeping. A city sound, not jungle. The bandit covering Vic pulled a Storm-reader from his back pocket, and tossed it to the one on Regina, saying, "Check it."

"Dang. Bad news, boys?" the recipient bandit said, baubling it open with one hand. "That's three since dawn. We gotta git."

The one standing on Jimmy's back looked up for a second. "Ain't see nothing yet," He said of the sky. As he weighted shifted, Jimmy twisted and made a reckless grab at the wrist holding the crossbow.

He found it. It broke it with a sideways yank. The bandit screamed out, and Jimmy rolled and pulled him down on top of him. He came up with the crossbow and pointed it at the leader. He ducked, pushing Vic down.

He yelped and bolted. The second followed, kicking Regina's knees from behind, swearing and brandishing the weapon until they were out of range.

As soon as they got the upper hand, Vic was yelling *shoot them, blast em up bruv, send it!*

As soon as he realized Jimmy was just pointing the weapon, not aiming, he lunged for it with a *gimme gimme, cummom bruv shoot them please shoot them,* his mind on the canister clutched beneath their leader's arm. But Jimmy stiff-armed his attempts and as they left site he tossed the bow in the dirt. Vic screamed in agony.

"Why!? Why dint ye shoot them bruv!?"

"True Zuri killeth not with coward-weapons, city-weapons. It is forebode."

"You coulda let me! Mate, yer fookin 'Touched. Dat was

our meal ticket! That was our fookin *life* you juss let run away!"

The man under the young barbarian stirred. Jimmy reached down and placed his thumb on a certain spot of his neck until he passed out. He shrugged.

"The Great Crow giveth, and The Great Crow taketh away."

XIV

Felix heard his friend draw breath, and braced for another plush sally of expletives, but Vic just exhaled.

"I... mate, I cant do nuffin wiff dat. Ye right, were partin ways. Yer fired."

He turned to Felix. "Lets juss git home."

Felix nodded. "We'll figure it out man, don't worry." but he realized he didn't believe himself by the time his sentence finished.

He looked around and down again, unable to bear the sight of anyone right then. They started moving towards their packs, dropped before the fight. Felix loved a good somber moment so it took a while to register, but it was there. A faint noise mixed into the wind. The woodlums were gone, but they could still hear the Storm-reader.

"Wait! Stop for a second." he said, hunkering his body. "Do you guys hear that?" everyone but Regina stopped crunching the underbrush.

Vic heard it. He did a double take at Felix, and then turned his head back towards her, a few steps ahead. Her hand was sliding into her pocket. The beeping was steady. The two roommates looked at each other, then back to her.

"Is dat—" Vic said. The wind whipped up.

"Okay! Yes yes yes, here, just take the effing thing, its not worth it!" she yelled, spinning around. "You two sadboys need it more than I do! I just want to get to the boat and never see you three again!" She pulled out the beeping box, flipped it into the air and ran back towards the path. Vic took off chasing her.

Felix caught the device, opened the lid, and read the dials. His eyes dilated.

"I knew it! I knew it!" Vic yelled after Regina. "Wot I tell you, Felix! Bare thieves on the Aeros! Lookat her, A chiselin, lowlife, sticky-fingered leech! Thats ye job? Pickpocketin workin folk? Oh! *So* much betta dan bein a Ranger, what good work ye do! Yeh, ye really give a shite about oppression. Fookin hypocrite, innit? Mebbe ye wouldna got yer ass pulled out of an Aero if ye hand werent in his *pocket!*" He yelled, catching up with her.

XV

Vic kept the beratement level high as they ran, and Jimmy jogged up with their packs on his arms. Felix wasn't far behind, feeling fresh motivation.

"UH GUYS WE REALLY HAVE TO HURRY." He said, catching up. He glanced at what the sky was saying. There was no strange glow yet, but the clouds were picking up speed, creeping the same way they were. Where trees parted he saw a thick pillar forming just ahead. His heart flailed. It was a system. Not a single cloudburst, a system, dead ahead.

They made it up the rise to the Crevasse fork before the thunder started and dark bruisy colors began to leak out of the clouds ahead. Vic didn't turn toward the overhang—they barreled down the hillside, down the path that lead to the river. Jimmy bringing up the rear was almost leaning on Felix's back. Their only hope was to get under the awning of the boatstop on the river before it broke loose. Felix realized that the Crevasse overhang had probably been closer, but the time to express that thought had elapsed precious moments ago.

They felt the second *THUD* in their chest a heartbeat after the first, as two cells of clouds burst together. The gale wind deepened and an unearthly light tinted their muddy footsteps.

They were at a dead race, running shoulder to shoulder, so when they collided with it, they all collided at once.

At one moment they were streaking down the last stretch, the puddles deepening into pools under their feet. The next moment, his head hurt, his feet weren't touching, he could feel them all smashing together, tangled with something against the ground. He thought for a second that was it, the Storm— but as he untangled, he felt feathers. He fell back and saw a flightless bird struggling up, beating its wings, and limping away across the path.

It was a shovelbill.

Pulling themselves up, he saw the look in Vic's eyes and just knew.

Felix yelled "No!" anyway, but he couldn't even hear himself. Vic was up, chasing the bird now, pulling the bow from his pack. Jimmy launched after him. Felix instinctively moved in the same direction, and felt a weight in the crook of his arm. It was Regina.

"What are you doing? We're about to get *'Touched!* Don't follow those idiots!"

"Keep your hands off me!" he yelled. "Do what you want, he's my friend!" She recoiled, and he dashed after Vic. There was still time, the sky above them was only a little orange—

He stumbled ahead for ten feet, and heard a keening squawk. Flashes of movement behind a tree. Jimmy was holding the bird's neck on the ground, throttling it. Vic was opening the transport container. There was an orange glint on his teeth. The storm meter was beeping so quickly now it was a solid tone.

"Guys, we have to go! It's going to happen!" he reached out to grab Vic's arm, and saw his limb wreathed in copper light.

And then nothing else could happen, because that was when his vision went and his ear drums emptied and a volcanic level of energy filled his earthly vessel.

XVI

There was no transition. He didn't feel himself rise in the air, but next he knew he was up there, moving steadily west like an outbound Aero, a half kilometer high. The whole Valley was splayed before him, no wet season fogs obscuring the view.

His body was flying without his input. He couldn't change courses or steer, only see. And something was wrong with his eyes.

The Storm had done something to his vision. It was like he could see too much. Everything he gazed at was reflected to him with such perfect fidelity, he could almost feel everything happening, down to each dew drop, as if it were happening on his own skin.

History would come to show that Felix had taken quite a good deal of drugs on his quest, and a variety to boot. This special site went beyond any chemical dissociative of mind or body, far beyond. It was like super-sobriety, the universe was lobbing cold hard bricks of truth at him from every angle. Plus, he could actually see others like he had been, taking said drugs, and felt what they felt too, as a limited subset of the greater feeling that was propelling him.

He few on, and realized he had crossed hundreds of kilometers in just a few second, taking him over the deep jungle now. If he looked back though, he could still see Heaven and every point in the rest of the Valley clear as crystal.

Sensory information soaked him like a rag. The range of faces he saw just in turning his head overlapped their teeth and merged their cries together in a dizzy kaleidoscope of humans in foreign and familiar and places.

He could see his sister's bedroom in Farseilles College, still empty, balcony door open letting smoke blow in. He glimpsed a huge throng of clay-caked archers at the top of the Crevasse, firing volleys down at something approaching from below. And in the jungle and on Heaven's turf alike, enormous fires roared and gave the sky grey banners that marked his progress as he plunged through them. Wherever his eyes touched confirmed that the Valley was not how he left it.

Everywhere, from the base of the cliffs to Heaven's lake, everyone were on the move towards desperate purposes. Huge groups of men, thousands there must have been, cloaked with leaves and ash to hide their blade's shine, moved through the forest, stalking each other. Just as many stood in Heaven's streets, alight in torchfire, a soiree of alarms and sirens echoing through the blazing streets. Wizards in trailing grounds flapped straight down from the upper ledges of burning College buildings, their metal frames buckling with heat and battery bomb blasts. Students bled out on the trimmed and trodden quads, under the fumy olive clouds that only came from burning solar panels.

He smelled and tasted, felt and heard it all. The Valley was unveiling itself to him, unburdening itself of dying worries in a great load. It fed in through his eyes and spray-coated everything inside. He could feel himself accelerating, and was far past any point on the map he had ever traveled to— he wasn't sure how he was seeing things and places he had never been, but he knew he coasted over snowy mountain plateaus running with floods, passing villages of yellow-eyed pygmies that stared up as he passed. He saw a bleeding sore in the sky above the skyline of a dark, cliff-carved city. His ears filled with noise and voices from every angle until it al became just a stream of audial salt. Vines and wires grew over ten meter gravestones, beneath a tree so large his brain must have been exaggerating.. A temple top glew slick with mixing blood. The taste of smoke on everyone's tongue. Everyone screaming out. All together.

He empathized with a million heartbreaks. He learned as many deeply dark facts as truth. He saw a host of soltions he had never dreamed of as he flew by. He felt the outer limits of his brain's capacity to know, truly felt what overwhelmed meant.

Dizzy, he looked at where he was heading for the first time. He had risen without knowing, higher than any Aero could climb, to be level with the obsidian cliffs that made up the Valley's untraversable western edge. On the cliffs lip were a set of bumps that he was flying directly toward. He tried to steer up, continue his unimpeded flight, but found out then he wasn't really flying at all. He was being pulled by something. Something stringing him along through the air with a set destination. He was still taking in impression after impression, but through them he tried to focus on the three little blips. The speed tried to force his head down and trying to maintain focus on one point almost blinded him. Pictures of the Valley's worst day kept rattling by, but he was sure, from that moment til the end—the three people on the cliffs, the ones who called them, they were screaming too.

The day came back like a punch to the temple. He was

on his back, looking at a normal sky, dampening to twilight, stars starting to show through the cloud breaks. His eyes could only see himself again. The shovelbill's blood flowed out in slow bumps of its dead heart. The creak and cry of the forest picked back up in the distance. His eyes hadn't been closed, but he wasn't sure how long he had been sitting there with them open. His head turned. Vic was sitting cross-legged on a log. He turned towards Felix with a bright look, like had had something smart to say, but instead his mouth opened and began to heave vomit out onto the rocks.

He saw Regina had followed them. She was on her hands and knees, breathing shallow, crackles of static foaming off her hair. She fell to her side and let loose a stream of gibberish, tongue not working. Jimmy slowly pulled his knees to his chest and began rocking himself.

Felix breathed. Looking at his companions, a feeling overtook him, one he didn't recognize. The world looked normal again, but strange now. Little details were standing out, whispering to him. The shocked stillness of the woodland around him echoed through him, but he was separate, himself. For the first time in a long time, he felt calm.

"No, no, no, no..."Vic was beginning to say, louder and louder, over and over.

"The Great Crow." Jimmy intoned to himself, thousand-meter staring at a rock.

"..*Flying*!" Regina finally managed, eyes alight. "We were flying! All flying!" she pointed at each like a child, with both fingers. Vic lolled his head and moaned.

"All fooked ye mean! Were all fookin broken in the head now. Fook." Vic said, scowling at his hands.

"We're not broken!" Regina cried. "We were soaring! Above everything!" she fluttered her arms a little, trying to regain the feeling.

"Dats *litrally* what dey all say— *uhhhg*." Vic said. His cheeks bulged with nausea again.

"Then they must all be right! Oh, eff— they're *all right*. So you two saw it too, right? We were flying, and then—"

Jimmy nodded. He turned to look west, at the great black cliffs.

Vic kept moaning *no* and shaking his head, refusing to listen. Regina grabbed Felix for stability.

"Felix! Tell him it was real! Tell him you were flying! Say what you saw!" her voice cracked shrill.

"Mate, dont do dis. Please, tell me ye see wots goin on."

Felix looked at them for a long second.

"I saw the Valley changing." he said.

"Great. You too. Were all gonna be gibberin maniacs in six months."

Regina's body shook. "Less for you, luv." He said.

"If it will even last that long. I think we saw how it all ends." Felix said.

"But we flew above it, so it's not doomed! We flew up there. There is something on the cliffs. That means there is a way to survive, whatever that was! Where do you think it comes from?"

"The Great Crow, she approacheth. Soon."

"And the three people at the end." Felix said. A chill ran down his spine.

"What?" Regina said."

"Oh no, no way! Dis is how it starts. No way. None of dat talk. Woteva it was, whereva its from, I ent lettin it git to me. You three can let ye brain turn to mush if ye want." Vic said.

Felix stood up, feeling light. He laughed. It was a real laugh he didn't control. It surprised him.

"Guys, I think you're all focused on the wrong things here."

"Im focused on how Im a freak now, and its only a matta of time before were screamin our head off in the street. Am I missin something?"

"Yes! I think so. Because we've never been 'Touched before, obviously, so how could we actually know? Everyone says the Storms make you dangerous and crazy. But look, we're fine. We're talking normally. I feel a little different, but not *crazy*."

"So?"

"So I think I just realized something. I don't think the Storm breaks people. I think it makes them see the city, or maybe wherever they're from, is broken, and needs to change, to avoid what the Storm showed us."

"Ye thought it was broken already, Felix."

"Yes, but I see it clearly now. I've been hating myself for as long as I can remember. Telling myself why I'm not good enough. Why I couldn't make it in the Colleges, why I can't hack it in lower Heaven. Why I'm barge-bait, because there's no other place for me." He looked down at his hands, then the backs of them, and his torso, and legs, as if realizing they were connected to his head for the first time.

"But I just saw it all falling apart. It's wrong, not us. It's going to happen, it can't not, I'm sure of it now. The Colleges, the Causeways, every system…its all ending. That's why there is no place for me, for any of us. This stress— we're not wrong, the City, the Rangers, my… the Wizards— they're all wrong! We're going to outlast them! It's beautiful."

There were tears in the bags under his eyes. He sniffed and closed his eyes and there it was again, the ending, with sureness. He opened his eyes to a *look* from Vic.

"Fook bruv, nice knowin ye I guess."

"Oh don't mope! Let's get up. Get that bird. We have things to do!" Felix said. Vic stared at his kill, recognizing it for the first time. Its feathers had sprung out golden in the storm.

"Come on, let's go!" Vic urged, waving them up with both hands.

"Alright, alright, flya— wots da rush?"

Felix looked at each of his friends, psyched out and worrying, not knowing how they would survive this, the latest in a series of little and big disappointments from life. From disparate corners, they had arrived here, to peer at one another from the silo of their own perspectives, unable to see how it all came together. He didn't either. But for the first time since he could remember, he was curious to find out.

He looked at his friends with eyes wide open.

"Our world, this world is ending soon! We have to be part of it! I don't want to miss a thing!"

Thank you for reading!
To tune in for more Lower Heaven action, follow
@lowerheavenbook on all social media platforms.
And feel free to shoot me a message about the
book or anything else! I respond to everything,
and would love to hear from you.
-Ben

*Ready for more? Read part one of Lower Heaven
Episode II: O Fortuna below:*

1

Vic gave his friend a moment.

"Wot mate, is dat supposed to be inspirin or someting?"

Felix fixed him with a look, still full of the apocalyptic surety they had all been blessed with by the Storm just moments before. Burning limbs toppled from their branches in the blast clearing.

"Your sayin youre all revved up for the downfall of society, all dat."

Felix considered this. "Yes! Yes I am! We just got a glimpse of the inevitable, the logical conclusion of, everything that is wrong with the City! I'm excited because that means we're not failures— of course we're failing, the whole thing is failing! We're not wrong to be behind in life, or suffering for it. And we're not alone. It's happening to all of us, and it's happening soon, how could it not, with the state of everything?? Everyone who is fighting for the way things are to continue are the crazy ones!"

"Slow eet down bruv, lowah ye voice."

Felix realized he was energized, shouting. He modulated his voice and thoughts.

"We have to make a plan. Figure out what we're going to do about this."

"Wot 'we,' bruv?" Vic panned to the other two. Regina was staring at the ground, pulling the hairs on one side of her head with both hands and conversing with herself, while Jimmy appeared was dropping into a crouch with a serious look on his face.

"He look like he's about ta take off inta da trees, and she's toast fa sure."

"Hey, don't do that! They're with us, at least until we get back. We all need to talk on the boat! Make a plan."

"A plan? A good plan is to act like it nevah happened mate, lookaddem." He pointed. "Dese man'll blab to the first mugs we see, get us effin sent in fa treatment."

"No, look, they're fine—"

"But we hardly know em, innit, cept she try an robbed us."

"The boatstop is just down the hill! We're all going the same way, stop being stubborn."

"Yeh, but fook if Im gettin onna same boat as her, specially now."

Felix let out a frustrated groan. "Vic, we have to parse what just happened! We're not crazy! We have to talk about what what we saw means!"

Vic probably would have had a remark for that, but the air lit up with a sound, a sharp pitch, dominating everything, one keening burst of high-end noise that arrived out of nowhere.

Felix startled upward, and clapped his hands instinctively over his ear drums. The wail undulated into a trill, a singing broken with pegs of silence, creating a flapping void in their ears like the air through the gap of an opening Aeromobile door. Felix spun to see who was attacking them and in a few seconds his eyes landed on Jimmy, mouth wide open, still hunched in a meticulous crouch. The shrill noise shrank as he ran out of breath, and as he pause to redraw it, Felix was on him with his hands in his face, and Vic was double-time packing up his things and securing the corpse of the Stormtouched shovelbill for rapid departure.

"Jimmy! Stop! Now!" Felix said. The young barbarian fixed him solemnly with his big brown eyes, welling with tears.

"What are you doing? Be quiet!"

"Singeth I the ancient mourn song of the White Crow tribe. One like me must now singeth."

"Okay, but everyone in a kilometer just heard that, so we have to go, like, now—" the barbarian raised his hand to say something else.

"Jimmy, I swear, if you say you will fight them all—"

"No. But I must tell thou a thing. All thou. Of import." He drew a serious breath, almost a sob, and began to explain.

"Can you summarize?" Felix said, searching the trees for lanterns. Jimmy looked at him hard for a second.

"I cannot."

"Alright, then it's really going to have to wait, Vic's about to leave us here— get your things. Get Regina, follow u
us!"

Vic was out already, fast-stepping back the way they came. Felix zagged until he was tromping level with his short friend.

The shovelbill had led them up a rocky crick they now scrambled back down, pushing through green and broken branches.

"Come on man, slow down, you're not going to leave us behind—they're staying with us!" Felix said.

"Bruv, why? We ent need em, dey on dey own ting! Dey'll get us nabbed bruv, blow our cova, blabbin and yo-delin on like dat! We gotta save ourselves, get back to our ends, juss lay low."

They found the main path, where many trails to far reaches all funneled the last few hundred yards to the boat-stop. Vic kept striding with effort.

"But what happened to us happened to them! We all saw the same thing, and we haven't talked about it! They're the only other ones we talk about this with!"

"Oosh, bruv, youre twisted! I ent talkin bout a Storm ting wif nuffin bruv. Serious."

"Don't do that! Don't shut down! You saw it, the vision, I saw you seeing it! And they did too! I am not proposing anything out of the ordinary, I'm just saying we need to agree to sit down and talk it through make a simple plan about how we are going to cope with this new knowledge, please!"

Vic stopped, reached out, and shushed him, as they had come within earshot of the little adventurer's rest at the riverfront.

He was clammed up by the silhouette of a man pissing into the river's reflected moon, and the shards of lantern light through the sides of the structure now visible. Vic looked at him stern, the skin around his weak eye twisted and squinty.

"Im not talkin bout it. I dont wanna be a flya." Vic said, before turning and stomping away towards the building.

Felix sighed, and waited a few seconds for his other companions to catch up.

II

The boatstop was a shack sat longways to the water, its hammered tin roof cocked up to offer sight of the river bend and sheet the elements away off waiting heads. A signal fire jumped out of a drum barrel lighting the one-boat boarding dock on the side open to the waterway. The Aeromobiles that dropped them in worked like windup toys—and there was no place to land and recharge in the jungle. The standard adventurer MO was to parachute in and hitch a ride back from one of the many makeshift stations on a boat bound for Heaven. Boats from upriver took on these passengers for a fare to earn a few extra coins for their troubles on the water. Wealthier adventurers splurged for flare packs that summoned on-demand cabskiffs and cut out the wait, but they were far from affordable.

Framed by four trunks still rooted in the riverbank, the ramshackle walls were timber slab aside reclaimed ship's planking, lashed in place or smacked to hold with fat square nails. A ring of patchy axe hacks and scorch marks made a clear yard around the structure. The forest crowded in quickly—it was seen as a civic duty for all level of jungle trawlers to maintain the little clubhouse's perimeter while waiting. A good way to blow off steam, too.

As they crossed the line really carved out from the rainforest, Felix pantomimed sewing his lips shut to Regina and Jimmy before stepping into the makeshift room. There was a fungal smelling must to the wooden shelter, sweat and anaerobic mud smell wafted up through the squishy boards. On their right hand the structure opened like a diorama to the river leg, their view fuzzed by a large flynet of gauzy mesh to stay the midge clouds. A bench facing the water ran the length of the dock—that was where Vic was, a silhouette pacing in front of the stoked drum fire. Inside, a small table had been knocked together, and a selection of stumps festooned the room. Those, plus one scratched-yet-ornate chair, its painted wood feet carved into dragon claws and lizards oiled onto the back, inexplicably here somehow in this rough place.

Two stumps and the chair were around the table, two young men sat the wooden rounds. The chair was empty, presumably for the man bravely relieving himself into the water's edge outside. The pairs' looks lifted as Felix entered with the two others, sharing an expression flat and dull as unscrubbed pans, eyes that had looked on too much today already. Both were blackened with dirt and singes, in matching beige vests cargoed with pockets. They were both missing big patches of hair, showing skin the florid mottled pink of flesh recently healed by health potion.

They nodded when they didn't feel threatened and turned back to their game of Iscosc, drawing triangular chalk marks between pebbles scattered on the table. This game, and the matching vests, which were borrowed from a lab closet somewhere, marked the two as Wizard students, either doing their Civil Service years or working towards a First Solvus by their age.

Felix looked to Jimmy and Regina, fearing a questionable outburst from either or both. Instead they stood transfixed, blinking around the shanty, seeing the man-made angles through their new lenses, as if born in the jungle that day. He felt it too—the stillness, the usual mundane peace of this place didn't match the flaming, urgent anxiety the Storm's rays had gifted him. Just being here, and thinking about his vision near other people put him on edge, out of place. Either something was deeply wrong with them all quietly going about their own unrelated business, or something was wrong with him. The feeling of the Storm was settled in, like another dark memory.

"Felix? Say, it is you!" Behind him another had come through the doorway.

He returned to his senses, then did a double take. The older man wore a set of old-timey eyebars that he'd recognize anywhere. The small metal ingots were held at his temples by wire looped behind the ears, they emitted a magical field, shaping the air to correct for flaws in the wearer's natural vision. Wrinkles parenthesized his wide bright eyes as if he were surprised to have reached middle age. He was slender, and wore one of those Wizard pocket-vests too, but his was of heavier cloth and tailored to his bony figure. Atop his head sat the characteristic tricorner hat, his had three stripes running around the brim, two barred green and the top purple, the highest noticeably newer than the other two. He leaned forward at the waist, and squinted to make double sure it was Felix.

Felix leaned in to Regina and whispered in a rush. "Go out to the porch, we'll talk out there. Wait for me, don't say anything to Vic, he's pissed off."

"Uh, why? This is his fault." Regina said, her tone challenging. At least the crazed look was receding.

"Please don't say that to him. He's para. Just don't. Jimmy's being weird too. Just, I'll be out in a second, go—" he usher-shoved her away, and turned back to the unlikely and awkward reunion he was about to have.

"Professor Ernst!" Felix blurted, cottoned for more to say.

"Felix! Long salutations! It is good to see you, my boy! I can't think of when last we crossed paths!"

"It was that time I dropped out."

"Ah, why, yes, it was. Dreadfulness. All understood though. These things happen, to some. But do not think of it, we are not studying history, how does your present treat you? You're in the jungle, have you made yourself a Ranger?"

"My friend Vic has. I am voyaging with him on my weekend. I work at Pagerock, in the boot department. I see you've achieved your Third Solvus... Plants? You switched departments?" Felix said, lifting his eye's to the Professor's hat, and skipping past any awkward pity he could have shown.

"Yes, and gratitude!" the older said reflexively, eyes pointing upwards as if he could see it. "I found a lot of intellectual fecundity in the thaumatic lichen study field — they're not very showy organisms, oft overlooked, one would say. But if you find the time to be fascinated with something no one else has been, discovery can be ripe. It avails that there are a myriad plethora of symbiotic relationships between plant and fungal species that produce variations in lichen, interactions going down to the mote and I theorize, to the submote level even."

"With chartable application?" Felix couldn't help but asking.

"Oh, yes."

The number of Solvi sewn around the conical head-piece denoted Ernst's achievement to the middle of the Wizard's pyramidal hierarchy— the Academocracy, the densely coiled organizational mechanism that studied the chaotic magic of the world and interpreted its forces into the knowable realm, transmuting their studies into the laws and policies that formed Heavenly civilization. The Academocratic system stretched all the way back to the days of the Founders early meetings. It put all of their lofty ideals of Merit, Logic, and Freedom into an actuality that governed all of the people on the island in the middle of the lake. The whole idea, as they all learned in History Class, was to lead to a better government than what the Old Continent had, which from all reports seemed to have been nothing but a series of arbitrary legal prejudices, roles and privileges assigned according to weird things like level of skin pigmentation, or second name, or even what you believed happened when you died. The Academocracy made all of that laughable. It replaced the old nonsense with a system that guaranteed free public education for all children, providing each the shape of their own destiny.

It started on the fifth birthdate, at the same time the child received their Social Identification Number. That made a space for them in the system, and put the kid on the roll for the next starting term. On the first day of the next dry season, the child was due at the Spire of Youth, by foot, bus, or autocart drop off, if their parents had the time. The second largest of the College pyramids, smaller only than the Edifice, its straight glass walls and ten circular floors loomed even larger than memory in the mind of all born Heavenites, the place they were made citizens. For ten hours a day, four days a week, for the next eleven years, the Academocracy took on the burdens of a parent to every registered boy and girl on the island, at great overhead cost to itself. Special childhood education Wizards ensured all youth learned the basic rules of society, starting at a young age with manners, response to authority, and when sharing was and was not appropriate. This tutelage grew to include language skills, and math, and the foundational tenants of Magic they would build upon later in their careers, as well as instruction in History and the civic rites of the place they lived, how to celebrate the Festival of the Free and other holidays.

They continued this widening dosage for just over a decade, rising a floor each year until at the very top of the Spire at age sixteen when the Learned Essentials Aptitude & Placement test was administered. This wasn't a pass-fail kind of test, no one was excluded from receiving more education, it was a sorting device. After taking the LEAP, the results were returned in a series of personalized recommendations for how best to advance one's life next, either continuing or exiting the system for better suited, economic pursuits in the City outside the walls and ungated entries of the College.

The nature of education changed after that point. After sixteen years of learning for its own sake, every study on was designed to be applied in the real world; broadly, to crafting the future leaders of the City. The next joinder towards becoming a full-on Wizard was five years of civil service (not to be confused with civic work, the purview of CWP recipients).

The island was ruled by a bureaucracy. Civil Service Interns filled the low echelons of the byzantine divisions and departments studying the clades of the world and controlling various municipal aspects. Five years of working one of these stipended positions was combined with continuing learning of Advanced Rudimentaries to hone their Magical thinking. These roles also served as an immune system for the Academocracy as a whole, ensuring idealists were cured of silly potential ideas while still inconsequential themselves.

After this final box of youth was checked, graduates were free to pursue the wide array of Wizard jobs available at the Colleges, and work their way upward through the departments. Mobility was built in, the inverted funnel of the Academocracy cuumed its talent upward through an equity-driven system of scheduled peer review. The higher one rose in the Departments the more interesting the work became, and the loftier the compensation in paid lodging within the college grounds, living stipends, and funded research lab time. The ultimate goal for most was obtaining a Sinecure— one of the upper to middle posts which deviated from the regular biannual position rotation, to ensure that the most important, tactic-setting roles were not constantly changing hands. These posts meant security for as long as you held good stead with one's peers and superiors, some of the choicest rewards for the Wizards who earned them through service and new discovery.

Solvi were a chart of the latter. Part of every position's compensation was lab time, and it was expected that in post-hours each Wizard was using such to develop and publish new studies of the world, developing new theories, turning Magic into applicable tech. Apart from being a consideration for applications to higher postings, a Wizard's stack of Solvi was his or her calling card, a flex of the brain on display to the rest of The Community, as Wizards referred to themselves.

Felix met Ernst when the professor only had two stripes on his hat and Felix was still part of said Community; Ernst's Applied Mammal Skull Formations lecture was one of his prerequisites. The spry teacher's ability (and tendency to) to orate the list of every bone in a vast number of animals' anatomies was part of his personal legend, as was the unflappable scruffiness and barely restrained obsession for street music. He took to it downright anthropologically, annotating the vulgar patois of lower Heaven in pulpy hobby journals that certain subcultures of Wizards subscribed to with hunger.

He became Felix's favorite teacher when they ran into each other at a grime rap battle in a club on Savion St. It was one of many sneakouts from the skydorm of his father that he still lived in, during his Civil Service years. Ernst claimed to be shirking a lab reservation. They both avowed to tell no one, and gleefully watched Stackt Papa absolutely bodybag Viciouz Zkinz, a huge victory for the Collusionaires, both of their favorite rap crew to make cheering sounds for.

That made him feel comfortable with Ernst because a professor who snuck out to rap battles obviously didn't care about impressing anyone, which was the type of Wizard Felix was angling to be. It had been a cinch since birth that his older sister, Kalix had been her name, was the intellectual heir apparent to their father's ambitious legacy. This had never been a problem for him, a total relief actually. He loved both of his family members dearly, and did not envy them for mentally superceding him, it felt natural and right and was comfortable. At that comfortable time, Felix still hoarded a childhood notion of training beasts for the Arena Pits, another oft-pursued hobby that could be a mid-level Wizard career arc someday. So he did his Civil time and early work years in the Biology department, slowly working toward the Solvus he'd never ended up getting.

The Bio Department, where Ernst taught and studied, regulated all flora and fauna entering the City at the higher levels, testing and watching for plague motes or other well-poisonings from hostile enemies of Heaven, heavy work. At lower levels (Felix's) Bio controlled the stray dog and cat population. He had hated that job too, but anything that wasn't a lateral move required at least one

Solvus out there, defended and recorded in the Vitae. He was working on animal lab science courses, but at his own pace, intermittently between nights carousing in lower Heaven, vicariously living a dark life, developing useless interests and habits.

His life before: dog nuts, lab classes, then hookah bars, Pit fight team drafts, salviasinte taprooms, food cart pods, sex-positive clubs, a regular schedule of trivia nights at assorted taverns, smoky billiard rookeries, sense cinemas, gaming lounges, a gorge of the whole wheeling complex of Heaven's lust to be entertained. Interspersed with weekly family dinners til the one week it didn't happen. Those nights he had used to listen about his sister and father's progress towards three and six Solvi respectively, upward through the Academocracy, this system to which there was no better alternative, which had perpetuated itself on its own merits for 225 years, inventing every paradigm-shifting technology their world had along the way, from the Cuum-can, to the health potion, to the Skyzymyk Solution, to the Aeromobile, with the vast promise of more to come.

"How amazing," Felix said.

"Indeed! I never thought I'd get my Solvo Tertio honestly, and much less in something besides marsupial osteography. The jump to a higher department level has left me with little time to stay abreast of happenings in the rap scene though, I say with sadness. I suppose we must all grow up eventually." He took on a startled look at his own words, like maybe he just offended Felix and was about to qualify his remarks.

Felix kept going. "Well, at least it still gives you reason to get out of the College, into the jungle, not all at your rank can say that."

"Ha! My wife wishes I was one of the ones who couldn't, she'd prefer I leave the danger to larger men. We were attempting to move towards more indoor, submote research work. But then came all this revelation over the adrenopomes and its just so hard to get clean lichen samples unless I source them directly."

"Adrenopomes? Like the fruit? In the Punica clade? We ran into some Rangers on the Aeromobile going for them this morning, has a new application been discovered by someone?"

"You haven't heard! Well I suppose you wouldn't have, oh, yes, it's been a saga these last few weeks, surely."

"What happened?"

"Well, I volunteered to be faculty sponsor to the two young ones there for this trip, and to collect some specimens myself, for an argument I am crafting. A fruitful voyage, ha! We got a wyvern too, quite beautiful. It may interest you, their research, not the wyvern, although yes, that too."

"...but of the pomes?"

"Oh, yes! I'm not sure if you recall from your time — there was an interesting-yet-ultimately-tangential argument being made about certain patterns found in the shells of Canlasian ink crabs affected by Pinyon Events."

Celio Pinyon, a prime descendant of the Founders, had been the first Wizard to make serious inquiry into the nature of the Storms, almost 200 years, 400 seasons, as the Zuri counted it.

"The proponents of this argument theorized any observable similarity that was a result of the Pinyon Events could potentially be the thread that could lead eventually to a useful understanding of the Events and their root. Their body of evidence never passed rigor, however, they documented hundreds of shells with no coherent pattern for every piece that did fit their test."

"It was a subject of the Plenary one year, wasn't it?" Felix asked.

"Yes yes, but that was even earlier. All of the proposed paths of research dried on the vine. Nothing was found that could be the basis for anything new. The only real result was a few months of disruptively high prices being paid for crab ink, which was annoying."

"So something has changed?" he said. The Professor laughed learnedly.

"Things can't help but not! But I supposed this thing is being remarked upon more than others... Let's see, I don't suppose you knew Werner Fewgaw, but he's a Wizard your age to watch up for, Edifice-bound for certain. He and his Botanicals cohort were apparently making an observation of what they thought to be the fruit of a new specie of tree. They were on an argument that the new specimen was in the same family as the adrenopome, as you know to be a marginally-useful-but-interesting plant, so a study was being made into this new thing's properties. When they cut the fruit laterally to observe the seeds, a great variety in placement was found, that corresponded with neither the size or weight of the fruit. After many of these, the cohort noted similarity of the pattern to those found on the crabs discovered years back. And based on that an argument emerged that—"

"The divergence of the new fruit was caused by the Storms!?" Felix incredulized. "But—"

"The plant kingdom has been previously thought to be unaffected by Pinyon Events, yes yes." the professor said, a bit miffed at having the punchline stolen by someone with less Solvos than he.

"This argument would seem to say that the changes have been more subtle in plants than animals, slow over the course of generations which we have been unable to note. Needless to say, several new lines of study have sprung from these new observations. Every page of the Botanical Codex is being scrutinized for similar signatures. Expect a higher bounty on any fruits or plants that look new— or that you've only seen in recent years... animals too... I hear myself and think it suffice to say just about everything with a trace of the Storm in it will be in extremely high demand again for the labs."

Felix wanted to change the subject, and at the same time became aware the other two men had stopped their game and were listening to this young outsider receiving attention from their superior.

"So you three were able to retrieve some specimens..."

"Yes, a beautiful ringtailed wyvern, and an excellent gathering of adrenopomes. Unfortunately the head was separated during capture, it would have been good to stuff and mount— almost perfectly preserved, and most undoubtedly Pinyoned."

"You see some significance in the tail patterns?"

"Hmm? Oh. No. Professor Patro was seeking more of the adrenopome cousins I told you about. It is his trip that I am sponsoring. Braznyn and Fallix here are his students. The wyvern was incidental to the course of study. It seems wyverns are particularly fond of the new specie however, which is notable."

"And so... where is Professor Patro then, Professor?" asked Felix, and he didn't even know why he was asking.

"Ah." Ernst face darkened momentarily. "In the Cuumcanister, with the wyvern. What's left. The Professor was... caught unawares, in his eagerness."

"But," he rejoined, after a second, "The pursuit of Logic will carry on, the wyvern and several bushels of 'pomes we garnered, from several trees, all catalogued now—what Patro gave us is a terrific contribution." He landed it with a flat, nodding smile.

Felix felt every blood vessel in his body go double time. He knew Ernst didn't remember what had happened to his sister. Three years ago was ancient history in the Community. But even at face value there was so little to respect about his words, Felix's imagination blackened at the thought of saying them.

And that was the trick to being a Wizard that Felix had never mastered, that detachment, the ability to see things removed from one another, the focus on parts in the abstract while ignoring the whole that allowed such a thought to be had. He tried not to show his revulsion. And Ernst now seemed to be thinking of a way to ask about his companions, so Felix tried to detach himself before it got worse.

"Well, I don't want to hold up your game any longer." He said. "I should talk with my cohort. It was good to see you again professor, I hope your studies progress well."

"Oh? Yes, you must, but before... I see you're traveling with a very...colorful party. Tell me, how has your Zuri been acting?" he lowered his voice slightly.

"He's not ours, we only hired him for the day. And fine. Normal. Why do you ask?"

"Oh, quite, pay no mind. It's nothing. Just that there are whispers... rumors, in certain College circles that something is building. In the Zuri quarter."

"A protest you mean? A riot?"

"Bigger. Something else. Something planned. Did he say anything strange? Seem on edge? Combative?"

"I haven't heard anything like that, Professor, and I live right next to the South Bank. Tell everyone there is nothing to worry about. Now—" Felix said, hoping he sounded sure of himself, trying to lead out of the conversation.

"Oh, right, yes, urm, well, good to see you my boy, til we — or rather, do be careful..." Ernst said, lowering his eye, sensing departure and sidling out of their dialogue with trailing abruption, giving him a true Wizard's goodbye.

OTHER WORKS BY FREE RADICAL BOOKS:

Lower Heaven: Episode II: O Fortuna – ISBN: 978-1078010818 – Buy Online

The Wizard of Boone's Book of Magick – ISBN: 978-1088487952 – Buy Online

www.freeradbooks.com

63117791R00078

Made in the USA
Middletown, DE
25 August 2019